A Dragon's Guide to the Care and Feeding of Humans

Laurence Yep & Joanne Ryder

Illustrations by Mary GrandPré

CROWN BOOKS
FOR YOUNG READERS
NEW YORK

Text copyright © 2015 by Laurence Yep and Joanne Ryder
Jacket art and interior illustrations copyright © 2015 by Mary GrandPré

All rights reserved. Published in the United States by Crown Books for
Young Readers, an imprint of Random House Children's Books, a division of Random
House LLC, a Penguin Random House Company, New York.

Crown and the colophon are registered trademarks of
Random House LLC.

Visit us on the Web! randomhousekids.com

Educators and librarians, for a variety of teaching tools, visit us at
RHTeachersLibrarians.com

Library of Congress Cataloging-in-Publication Data
Yep, Laurence.
A dragon's guide to the care and feeding of humans / Laurence Yep & Joanne Ryder ;
illustrations by Mary GrandPré. — First edition.
pages cm.
Summary: Crusty dragon Miss Drake's new pet human, precocious ten-year-old
Winnie, not only thinks Miss Drake is her pet, she accidentally brings to life her
"sketchlings" of mysterious and fantastic creatures hidden in San Francisco,
causing mayhem among its residents.
ISBN 978-0-385-39228-0 (trade) — ISBN 978-0-385-39229-7 (lib. bdg.) —
ISBN 978-0-385-39230-3 (ebook)
[1. Dragons—Fiction. 2. Imaginary creatures—Fiction. 3. Artists—Fiction.
4. Magic—Fiction. 5. Friendship—Fiction.] I. Ryder, Joanne.
II. GrandPré, Mary, illustrator. III. Title.
PZ7.Y44Dqs 2015 [Fic]—dc23 2014017803

Printed in the United States of America
10 9 8 7 6 5 4 3 2 1
First Edition

To Gail Collins,
who brought us together,
with our thanks

A Dragon's Guide
to the care and feeding
of Humans

CHAPTER ONE

~~~~~

If you value your happiness and sanity,
take your time and choose your pet wisely.

It was a lovely funeral for Fluffy, the best pet I ever had. I was pleased by the turnout at the mansion. Mourners filled the large backyard and mingled as the sun finally broke through the San Francisco fog. Everyone had loved Fluffy. She had such a gentle temperament— quite the nicest of all my pets. Even when she was feeling out

of sorts, she never bit anyone—partly because I had trained her well and partly because she wouldn't hurt a fly.

She was such a special pet that I knew I could never find another one like her. I intended to bide my time, perhaps sleep for twenty or thirty years, until the ache in my heart had eased a little. Even then, I wasn't sure when I would get another pet.

But Winnie didn't give me any choice. Just two days after the funeral, she stomped into my lair. Without any warning, I heard a key scraping against the lock; then the door jerked open. The little creature stepped inside. She was the scrawniest of specimens, dressed all in black. Her very curly, every-which-way hair was light brown.

Putting a fist on her hip, she studied me, her glance flicking from the tip of my tail to my glorious head. "Are you really a dragon?" She sounded disappointed.

"Don't be rude," I snapped. "And how did you get the key?"

"Great-Aunt Amelia put it in her last letter to me," she said as she strolled farther inside my living room. Amelia was the ridiculous nickname that the other humans used for my Fluffy. "It had directions to the hidden door in the basement." She stared at me bold as brass. "She was afraid you'd be lonely."

"Well, I'm not." I held out my paw to the obnoxious creature. "So give me the key and go away."

Instead, she circled round my lair, stopping by the Regina and the metal song discs. She looked curiously at the large box, which was some two feet on each side. Delicate wooden inlays created lovely pictures of coral and shells on its lid, front, and sides. "What's this?"

"A music box," I said. It had been a gift from Fluffy's grandfather Sebastian, who had been fun when he was young but had become terribly boring when he grew older. Still, he had never been stingy, and the music box had been only one of many expensive presents.

She pivoted slowly. "I thought a dragon's den would be different."

"I dare you to show me a nicer one," I sniffed.

She waved her hand at the floor in disappointment. "I figured you'd have gold and jewels lying around in piles, not a carpet and a sofa."

"Have you ever tried sleeping on gold?" I asked. Then I answered my own question because I knew she didn't know. "Gold is hard and cold, and as for jewels . . . well . . . the diamonds leave scratches on my scales that take forever to buff out."

If this fussy little thing had had any manners, she would have stifled her curiosity, but she was obviously quite feral. She motioned to the red velvet drapes with the tassels of gold wire. "Okay, then why do you need curtains? You're underground." Crossing the room quickly—her shoes tracking dirt all over the best Bokhara wool, woven by a master weaver—she jerked a drape back to reveal the painting before I could stop her.

"Huh," she said, surprised, and then leaned forward to examine it closer. "What's this doing here?"

Perhaps she had been expecting some oil painting by a celebrated artist instead of a child's crude water-color, but I wouldn't have traded it for ten Rembrandts. A dragon with shining crimson scales soared into dark, dark clouds from which lightning bolts shot like jagged swords. A few years ago, Fluffy claimed she had found it at a holiday sale run by the parents of the Spriggs Academy students. She said that it had reminded her of me, so she had put it into a lovely gilded frame—Fluffy always had exquisite taste—and presented it to me.

And I'd been just as enchanted. The young artist had painted the red dragon with fiery eyes and a determined jut of her jaw as her powerful wings fought the winds. It was just the way every dragon should be.

"Get away from there," I said as firmly as any dragon could. But she wasn't listening.

She rubbed at the little spot of steam her breath had

4

left. "The glass protects it. But even if I smudged it, I could always paint you another."

I gazed scornfully at this preposterous creature with the unruly hair. "Don't be absurd."

She rounded on her heel. "I sent it to Great-Aunt Amelia four years ago."

"It came from a school sale," I insisted, but I was less sure now. I had never been able to break Fluffy's habit of telling little white lies.

"Turn it around." The creature jabbed her finger at the painting. "I wrote my letter to her on the back."

I decided to call her bluff. "If your writing isn't there, will you leave?"

She folded her arms confidently. "Sure, but I get to stay if it is."

The painting hung from the picture molding that ran parallel to the floor and high up on the wall. I lifted the frame upward, unhooked the wires from the molding, and tore the brown paper from the back.

There, written with a pencil, were a child's crude block letters:

DER ANT AMELEEA,
   I LIKE YUR STOREES. MAMA REEDS THEM 2
ME LOTS.

It was signed: W.

A bony finger pointed at the signature. "The 'W' stands for Winifred. That's me."

"Fl—" I caught myself. "Amelia told you about me?"

To her credit, Winnie traced Amelia's name sadly. "I thought the dragons in her letters were imaginary. But I loved hearing them, and later, when I could, reading them myself. It was great when I found a letter in our mailbox." She lifted her head to look at me. "Then her last one was sad but wonderful too. She told me you were real and where to find you."

Fluffy, Fluffy, what have you done? She had told me that she was leaving the house to a niece and her daughter and had taken care of everything. I assumed that Fluffy had drawn up a will. I had no idea she had gone so much further.

I set the painting down on the floor. "What did she tell you about me?"

"She said you'd ask but that it was better to keep you guessing or I'd never get the upper hand." She plopped down on the sofa and stroked the plush cushions. "This is more comfortable than it looks." I could see she would be rather impossible to train.

With a claw, I wrote the word *tsäm,* and from the last letter, I drew an ever-widening spiral as I muttered the spell. The world disappeared in a shimmering haze as I swelled to twice my comfy-at-home size. When the haze cleared, she seemed suitably impressed.

My head grazed the ceiling as I stared down at her. "Tell me the stories she put in her letters," I growled, and made a point of showing my gleaming white fangs and sharpening a claw on a chest scale. I waited for the appropriate screaming, groveling, and begging me to spare her.

Her eyes did widen, as if she was finally realizing how dangerous I could be, but she didn't shriek or drop to her knees in terror. Instead, she stayed put on the sofa. "No," she said with a quaver in her voice.

I leaned forward and pointed a claw at the door. "Get out."

She gasped and then stared at me, eye to eye. "In her letter, Great-Aunt Amelia also asked me to visit you. She said you'd be so sad that you might hurt yourself."

I was so startled that I sat down on my haunches, not knowing whether to laugh or cry. That sounded like my Fluffy. Even as she was dying, she was more concerned about me than about herself. But she was also always getting things wrong—the First One bless her. I would no more hurt myself than I'd give up tea.

I wiped a tear from my eye with a claw. "No, I'm quite all right, as you can see. So please leave."

She stared at the tear on my claw as it solidified into

an iridescent pearl. Her mouth opened in a little O as the reflected light bathed her face in shimmering rainbows. So *some* magic dazzled her.

I thought she was one of the greedy humans, so I offered the gem to her as a bribe. "Here. Take this and don't come back or tell anyone."

She draped her arms behind the sofa. "I don't want *that*. I want *you*."

Her audacity left me speechless for a moment. There are dragons who would have bitten her head off for the insult—as if a human could ever possess a dragon. "Well, you can't have me."

"Sure, I can," she said. "My mom got Great-Aunt Amelia's mansion, and I got her 'guest.'"

I was going to pound my head against the wall but caught myself just before I put my skull through a painting and smashed a few of Monet's water lilies. *Fluffy, Fluffy, what were you thinking? But of course, you weren't really thinking, were you?* "She put me in her will?"

Winnie noticed my clasped paws and realized I was upset. "Don't worry. That was also in her last letter to me—Mom got her own letter about the house but not about you," she added hastily. "Great-Aunt Amelia's place looked nice in the photo, but I didn't realize how huge it was until we got here. It's awesome! And for the first time in my life, I have my very own room. Can you believe it?"

"You never had your own room before?" I asked.

"Nope. I usually slept in part of a living room." She crossed her legs. "But now my room just goes on and on. I love it! I wish I could thank Great-Aunt Amelia somehow. We didn't know what we were going to do after a temperamental horse Mom was riding bucked. She fell and hurt her leg, and the doctor told her she shouldn't ride right away."

Though I believe the old ways are better, even I knew humans had replaced horses with cars that let them irritate more people with their noise and smells. After all, why annoy just your neighbors when you can annoy an entire state? "What was she doing on a horse?"

"Anything and everything she could," Winnie explained. "She was a practice rider for racehorses, but she also gave riding lessons, took care of horses, trained some . . . you name it. We lived in a *lot* of places."

Winnie's mother, Liza, was the daughter of Fluffy's brother, Jarvis, who'd been a prig and a wretched little sneak as a boy. Amelia was my pet, but *he* most definitely was not. I'd perfected some of my spells avoiding him in the mansion.

It was a great relief when he'd grown up and moved

to the East Coast years ago and become wealthy in his own right.

I took a closer look at Winnie. She had Amelia's broad forehead and Winthrop's bright blue eyes. That happens when you raise humans as pets. Sometimes you see the ghost of an old friend staring at you from the face of a stranger.

"Why were you living like Gypsies?" I asked.

"My grandparents didn't approve of anything Mom did—whether it was riding horses for a living or marrying my dad." Winnie grimaced. "When Dad died, my grandfather tried to take me away from her because she had to work all day and leave me alone. He said he had the money to take care of me."

It was my turn to frown. Leave it to Jarvis to hound his own child and granddaughter. I suspected that Liza had moved from state to state, not to change jobs but to keep one step ahead of the courts and her father. I hoped Jarvis gnashed his teeth to nubs when he heard that Amelia's inheritance had gone to them, especially since it protected them from his taking Winnie. "Well, he can't bother you now."

"It's all like a dream," she said, almost whispering. "We got here yesterday, and I just sat and stared out my window at the bay—at the boats, at the big yard all around. It's a bigger yard than I've ever seen, bigger than any of the others in the neighborhood."

"The other houses weren't around when the mansion got built," I said.

"By Great-Great-Great-Grandfather Winthrop?" she asked. "I'm sort of named after him."

Ah, dear Winthrop! I called him Lucky, because that was what he was, after wandering away from his father's hired riverboat and into the Malaysian jungle. I'd found him in the gully where he'd hurt himself in a fall and felt sorry for him. So I'd disguised myself as a human and brought him back to his parents, who were collecting plants for the Royal Botanic Gardens at Kew in England. His parents knew everything about plants and nothing about anything else. They would have wandered into the bandit ambush if I hadn't saved them. Their helplessness amused me, and their curiosity and cheerfulness charmed me, so I stayed with them until their expedition ended. One thing led to another, and I wound up here, thousands of miles from any land I had known, in America.

"Was he surprised to find out you weren't human?" she asked.

"I showed him my true shape about a month after I met him," I replied, and added, "He displayed the proper sense of awe—unlike his present descendant."

"I know all about dragons," she said. "I did a report on dragons at my last school. The books say Western dragons breathe fire and Eastern dragons cry pearls. So you're an Eastern dragon, right?"

"*Humph,*" I said. "What dragon wrote those books?"

"People wrote them," Winnie said. "I never read a book by a dragon."

"That explains why they are wrong," I told her, my paw thumping the table. "I know Eastern and Western dragons who can do both. As a matter of fact, so can I. Each dragon is unique. Some are more magical and learned than others. We choose to be who we are, and I choose to be the best dragon"—then I corrected myself modestly—"the best dragon I can be."

"Wow," she said. "And you're mine."

At that moment, I was one froggy hair from switching to barbecue mode when I was thunderstruck, absolutely *gobsmacked* by a thought. *Was this how my Fluffy thought of me? As hers!* I was speechless. It was so outrageous that it was beyond belief.

"Can I see you change into a human?" Winnie asked hopefully.

"Little girl, do I look like a magic show?" I said sternly.

"I'm not little. I'm ten," she said indignantly.

"And I am three thousand years old," I said. "Show some respect."

She leaned her head to the side. "You don't look a day over three hundred."

She was grinning, so I couldn't be sure if she was complimenting me or teasing me. "Thank you, I guess. Now, I'll take that key." I held out my paw. When she didn't move, I added a warning. "I'll hold you up by an ankle and shake you until the key drops out."

She tossed me the key with a smirk. "Take it. I made a dozen copies before I came down here."

As she closed the door behind her, I couldn't help thinking that she was a clever little creature for a mere hatchling. But she was going to find that in a game of wits, she was playing on my board with my pieces and my rules. My victory was a foregone conclusion. It just remained for her to wave a white flag in surrender.

CHAPTER TWO

To train your pet, you will need three things:
Patience, Patience, and, above all, Patience!

I toyed with the idea of barricading the door. But if the other dragons heard I was hiding from a ten-year-old human, I would be the laughingstock of the Seven Seas. So instead, I wrote on a sheet of foolscap in my neatest paw-writing:

Stay Out.
This Means You, Winnie!

I knew she could read, so if she ignored the sign, I would have to make it clear to her that she was not welcome. A firm paw,

after all, is the key to dealing with humans, who are over ninety percent monkey—and there is no paw firmer than mine.

Satisfied, I pinned the sign to the front of the door and tried to put the bothersome little creature out of my mind while I considered my other problem.

The email inviting me to the Enchanters' Fair had arrived just before Fluffy died. The largest magical festival of the year was now just a couple of days away, and I had to make a decision about whether to take part or not. As I was a founding member of the festival as well as the reigning Queen—a title I earned every year by winning the major magical contest of the Fair—the other magicals would expect me to attend and enter again. They wouldn't understand why I would mourn for a natural, as we called humans—only my friends would sympathize.

So I decided against making a token appearance, because once I was there, I would be unable to resist competing in the Spelling Bee. Expanding my knowledge of ancient spells was my passion, and I was never averse to a challenge.

I thought of the sorceress who considered herself my greatest rival. "You've always wanted to be Queen of the Fair, Silana," I murmured. "Congratulations."

I was just typing a polite email to the Fair committee when the door opened and Winnie entered.

15

I should have known a sign only works for someone with a minimal sense of courtesy.

"I brought some checkers," she announced, holding up a cardboard box.

I pointed at the front door. "Didn't you read my sign?" A new thought came to me. "Or can't you read cursive? Should I have written in block letters?"

"I can read cursive perfectly well—even if *you* do use too many curlicues," she said, tracking dirt over the Bokhara again on her way to the dining table. "Great-Aunt Amelia said you like to play games. I'll even let you cheat."

I thumped my tail angrily, and when I saw the cloud of dust rising from my carpet, I realized I needed to clean my rooms again. "I do not cheat."

"Great-Aunt Amelia said you'd say that." From the box, Winnie took out a piece of folded-up butcher paper. When she spread it on the tabletop, I saw that the squares had been hand-drawn and the border decorated with crude crowns, unicorns, and lions.

"Where did you get that?" I demanded.

"I made it." She began to take out checkers cut from cardboard and colored with crayons. "We never had much money before, and we were always moving around. So my set was cheap and easier to pack."

"Well, you have a permanent home now," I assured her. So had her great-aunt Amelia and all of Winthrop's descendants.

After a rootless childhood of tramping around the world with his scientist parents, Winthrop had been delighted to have a place that would always be his—or rather, ours—for as long as I chose to stay.

With the help of my pearls, we'd built this fancy lair over 140 years ago, and then I'd used more pearls to set up a trust fund that would maintain the house and grounds as well as provide generous allowances to the tenants like Winnie and her mother. Winnie should be able to buy any toy she wanted, so why was she still using a homemade one?

"Don't you have the money to purchase a new set of checkers?" I asked. "Or perhaps your mother hasn't had time to take you shopping?"

She began to set out the pieces, even though they slid about because she could not get the paper board to lie flat. "I told Mom this works just as well as a new one."

In the corner of the board, I saw a *W* and an *A* inside a big heart. "I assume 'W' is Winnie, but who's 'A'?"

"Andrew, my dad," she said, refusing to look at me.

I thought of a younger Winnie—hopefully with her hair actually brushed—coloring the pieces her father had cut from cardboard. "There are some things you can't replace," I observed.

"He was a real artist," she said softly. But his death must have been a painful memory because she didn't give me a chance to ask about him. "I'll even let you go first," she said brusquely. "You can be red."

I had intended to lift her by the collar of her ragged T-shirt and toss her back out into the basement—and then wash my paws with strong soap—but instead, I sat down and used a claw to move my first piece.

"It's funny that Amelia never told me that she was writing to you," I said, trying to sound casual.

Winnie leaned over so all I could see was the top of her head as she shifted a piece to another square. "It didn't matter where we had moved to, somehow her letters always reached us. Money, too, even though we never asked for it."

That sounded like my sweet Fluffy. I fought the urge to cry because cleaning up the pearls can be such a nuisance. Humans have it so much easier when they weep. Still, my vision was a little blurry when I moved a piece.

"You just went two spaces," Winnie said, "but I said I'd let you cheat today."

"That's quite *generous* of you," I said sarcastically.

"I know how it feels when you lose someone you love," Winnie said.

And I knew she meant her father. The strange little creature was trying to comfort me in her own clumsy way. It was just the sort of kind impulse that I had loved in Fluffy—though, of course, Fluffy would have been far more graceful doing it. But then, Fluffy had grown up in a world shaped by etiquette and with everything that money could buy, instead of moving around and having to make her own toys. But I was being disloyal to Fluffy's memory, so I switched to other topics.

"You didn't seem very surprised to see me in my true form for the first time," I said as we went on playing. Fluffy hadn't been either. And I had loved her all the more for that. In my experience, it's a rare human who can accept you for who you truly are.

"I've always wanted to meet a real dragon," she said. "My dad knew everything about them, so he was forever telling me stories about them."

"He was an expert on dragons?" I asked. That would have made him very special among humans.

"Well, he was always reading about them," she said, "and then making up stories."

I almost slammed my paw on the board. "Do I look imaginary to you?"

"Of course not," she said. "Who'd ever make up a dragon as grouchy as you?"

As she squinted at the board, studying her next

move, her fingers rubbed against a silver medal hanging around her neck—it looked old-fashioned, embossed with a winged foot, the symbol of the god Mercury.

"Is that your good-luck charm?" I asked, trying to change the tone of the conversation.

"Yes," she said. "My father gave it to me. His grandfather won it for the high jump. He was a fireman and the best athlete around."

"Firefighters are noble folk," I said, glad that her father had come from such stock.

"I know," she said. "My dad always wore it to honor him, and now I do too . . . and it does bring me good luck."

Suddenly she began to leapfrog a piece across the board to the end. "King me," she said as she took away my pieces.

I stared down in dismay at the gap in the center of my defenses and a king ready to rampage in the rear of my lines. "I thought you said you were going to let me win today?"

She picked up one of the pieces I had taken and kinged her piece herself. "I said I'd let you cheat." She grinned up at me. "But that doesn't mean you're going to win."

I shifted in my chair, finding a more comfortable position while I figured out my next move. "You asked for it. Don't cry when I rain down death and destruction on you."

"Oh, I'm shaking in my boots," she said mockingly.

As I studied the board, I couldn't help grumbling, "You really ought to be scared of me, you know. I'm a dragon; I have teeth, I breathe fire. I could singe you to a crisp."

She looked at me seriously. "I am afraid, but not because you might bite or burn me. I think you could do a lot more damage with your tongue than you would with your fangs and claws."

I leaned my long neck to the side to study her from another angle. "Are you really only ten?"

She shrugged. "Mom says I've gone through a lot more than most ten-year-olds should."

I thought about those words, maybe too much so, because she won not only that game but five more. Even Winthrop had never been able to win more than two games in a row from me—and I did not cheat him either!

"That's enough cheering up for one day," I said. "I can only take so much losing."

She raised her arms over her head in victory and then rocked from side to side. "Great-Aunt Amelia wrote that you served her tea and cookies after a game."

"Your great-aunt Amelia had better manners," I sniffed.

Winnie lowered her arms. "You mean she let you win. Don't be such a bad sport."

"I'll have you know that I won on my own," I snapped. "And anyway, I ran out of tea this morning."

Winnie couldn't hide her disappointment. "Not even those little cookies shaped like flowers?"

"My cupboard is quite bare," I insisted. I hadn't felt much like shopping after I lost Fluffy.

"Well, it's time for me to go anyway," Winnie said, looking at the French timepiece on the marble mantel. "Mom's still recovering from her fall. If I don't watch her, she'll forget to rest."

I was thoughtful as she lifted the handmade board and poured the pieces into the box. "You take care of her, do you?"

"And she takes care of me. It's always been me and her against the world." She folded up the board and stored it away. "Sometimes she held down two jobs just so we'd have a place to live and something to eat. But now we got this house and plenty of money, so I can watch over you too." When she stood up, Winnie fished a key from her pocket. "Want to add this one to your collection?"

"What would be the point," I asked, "when you have all those other copies?"

"Maybe I lied yesterday." She dangled the key between her fingers. "Maybe this is the only extra one."

Winnie was more pest than pet. "Do you ever stop playing games?" I demanded.

"You may hate to lose, but I *love* to win," she said as she left.

I stared at the door long after she had gone. I would have to take responsibility for her whether I wanted to or not. But I had raised enough pets to know that some of them needed to be challenged before they became bored and got into trouble—and I could see a creature like Winnie burning San Francisco down.

For Fluffy's sake, I would see she got a good education at an extraordinary institution of learning like the Spriggs Academy—which might at least keep her from destroying the city.

CHAPTER THREE

❧

Always make sure your pet knows who's in charge.

The next morning, I disguised myself as a human and put my pearls into a large purse. Then I headed into my exit tunnel, lead-ing under the lawn, away from the mansion, under several blocks, and up into a shed in a grove in a park. But when I reached the door at the end, it wouldn't budge. Peeking from under the door was a pale

scrap of paper. Though the tunnel was dark, it was no darker than the seafloor, where sunlight never reaches and dragons glide freely, so I had no trouble reading the scrawled message.

The note said:

ASK POLITELY AND I'LL UNLOCK THE PADLOCK
ON THE OUTSIDE OF THIS DOOR.
    WINNIE

A touch of spirit in a pet is one thing, but this was quite another. I crumpled up the note, angry at her insolence and even angrier at the threat to my freedom.

How dare she try to play tricks on me? I'd sneak out of the house and finish my shopping. When I came back, I'd snap the padlock from the exit door, and then teach Winnie not to trifle with a dragon.

As I stormed along my escape tunnel, I changed my revenge to a stern scolding. After all, the whole trip was for her sake. But when I stepped into my apartment, I found that another note had been slipped under my front door.

This one said:

CALL ME.
    WINNIE

As if I'd let her tell me what to do.

With a snort, I tried to open the door and found it wouldn't move either. She must have padlocked that door too. I had half a mind to smash the door to kindling, but I didn't know how much Winnie's mother knew about me. She might have heard the noise and come to investigate.

So instead, I picked up my smartphone. There was a note taped to it with a number.

I dialed, but she didn't pick up until the ninth ring. "Hello, Miss Winnie's residence."

"Don't you 'Miss Winnie' me," I snapped. "Open my doors."

"What's the magic word?" she asked.

"You are overdue for a spanking," I threatened.

"That's more than one word," she informed me, "and none of them are very magical."

I caught myself just before I crushed the telephone into dust. The main thing was to get out of here quietly. "Please," I said through gritted teeth.

"See how easy that was?" she asked cheerfully. "So where are we heading?"

"*I* have to buy some tea," I said sternly, "and I will do so alone."

"We'll see," she said slyly. "I'll meet you by the exit door."

It took her a half hour to open the door of my escape route and allow me to step out of the shed in the park. As I shouldered the purse's strap, she stared at my up-turned nose and short, bobbed blond hair. I was of an undetermined age, not too young, not too old . . . just in the prime of life.

I've taken on many human forms in my day, but for the past hundred years or so, I had usually modeled myself after a French girl I had met while traveling with my pet Orlando. Jeanne had been very sweet and made the most wonderful cheese until the day she fell from the loft in her family's barn. Even though her bones had healed nicely under my care, she'd started hearing voices telling her to save France from the English. I'd always regretted that I hadn't sat on her until the fit had passed because it had all ended very badly for her.

"I'm Miss Drake," I said. "That's an old word for 'dragon.'"

"Not very inventive," she sniffed.

"I don't use the wrong name that way," I said. "It's easy to get confused when you've had as many identities as I've had."

"Just how many fake identities have you had?" she asked curiously.

"As many as I've needed," I said, and held out my gloved hand. "I'll take that padlock."

She passed the padlock to me, and I had the satis-faction of seeing her eyes widen as I crushed it in my hand. "Don't ever lock me inside again. Now go home and open up the door to my quarters."

"I promise," she said. "Just as soon as we return from wherever we're going."

"I thought you said you had to keep an eye on your mother?" I asked her.

Winnie folded her arms and shrugged. "Mom's get-ting some physical therapy. She told me to stay here be-cause it would be boring."

I sensed that Winnie was feeling a bit lonely in her new home. Perhaps a jaunt outside would do her some good. "You can come if you give me your word you'll be quiet."

She drew an invisible zipper across her mouth. "You won't even notice I'm there."

I doubted that. Winnie would always make her pres-ence known. "How did you know where my exit door was?"

"Great-Aunt Amelia's journal had a map," Winnie said. "She put it in her last letter. She said it would help me get to know you."

"Journal? What journal?" I demanded. It was news to me that Fluffy had been keeping one. "Your great-aunt never told me."

"Maybe she wanted a little privacy," Winnie said.

"Well, I wish you'd destroy that journal," I said, and to be sure she would do it, I added, "Please."

"Not a chance." She looked around the little grove of trees that grew around the shed at the center of the park. It sat upon the peak of a hill and was a square about a block on each side. All around us the lawn stretched down the slopes to the surrounding streets. "It's amazing that no one ever found your door besides Great-Aunt Amelia."

"There's a charm that keeps people away," I said, pointing to the yellow piece of paper with the spell that I had written in the special dragon script. It was also why this was the one spot in the park that was never littered with empty soda cans and potato chip bags. "Amelia knew about it only because I led her grandparents through it after the mansion collapsed in the Great Earthquake. Her father, Caleb, was only a young child then, and I carried him myself."

"When did it fall down?" she asked.

"In 1906." I waved a hand toward the eastern half of San Francisco. "We stayed here with a lot of other refugees, so we saw the fires start to burn what was left of the city. The smoke turned day into night, and there was a wall of flame slowly marching over the hills. I was just a whisker away from taking my true form and flying Caleb away. But the firemen, soldiers, and sailors fought the fires to a standstill and then put them out."

As I stood on the hilltop, dragon-egg-blue sky all around me, I could feel the wings itch beneath the skin on my back, wanting to spread wide and fly.

When we left the park, Winnie asked, "Where are we going?"

"Shopping," I said.

"But downtown's that way," she said, waving toward the east.

I set a brisk pace, hoping that she would have to save her breath for walking rather than talking. "What would I want with the bright trash they sell there? It's fit only for"—I almost said "humans" but caught myself in time—"magpies. I take my custom to establishments that cater to creatures of more refined and elegant tastes."

She drew her eyebrows together as if she were translating my sentences. "Are there really shops for dragons?"

"Of course," I said, but good manners also made me add, "and the other magicals too."

I could see in her eyes that she was growing excited, but she made a big show of not caring. "You mean, there are other magical people in San Francisco?"

"More than you know." I laughed. "A mountain

nymph may live for free in her cave, but she still has to eat. Perhaps she becomes a waitress or street singer for part of the day. You can never be sure when you meet someone for the first time—which is why it's always wise to be polite."

"You weren't very polite to me," Winnie claimed.

I tapped the side of my nose. "I could smell that you were trouble right away." I paused and leaned over her solemnly. "Promise me that you won't tell anyone about me or about all this—not even your mother," I said as sternly as I could.

"Why?" Winnie asked.

"Once, dragons and other magicals lived openly with humans," I explained. "Sometimes it worked out fine, like it did for dragons in China. We were usually treated there with respect. But in Europe, people assumed dragons would burn down their homes and grab the nearest person for supper. For them, the only good dragon was a dead one."

Winnie wrinkled her nose in disgust. "That's awful."

"Dragons weren't the only ones who were mistreated," I went on, "so the different magicals agreed to keep their powers secret or hide from humans altogether. Over the centuries, we've done such a good job that most humans consider all us magicals imaginary."

"But you showed yourself to Great-Aunt Amelia," Winnie said.

"If we're careful, we're allowed to reveal the truth to a few special humans like your great-aunt Amelia," I said. "But other humans can't know, or we could both be in big trouble."

"How much trouble?" she asked curiously.

"Lots," I said. "So much that you and I will wish we had never been born."

She stared up at me defiantly. "You can't scare me."

"Probably not," I agreed, "but what would your mother do without you?"

That made her hesitate. Finally she shrugged. "Well, Great-Aunt Amelia told me to keep you a secret. I guess I can go along with it for now."

As we entered the lobby of a ten-story glass-and-chrome building, she looked around. "The shops are in a hospital?" she asked. At least she had enough sense to speak softly.

"Don't be so thick," I said, heading for the elevators. "I can hardly take my true shape in the park, but no one will notice me transforming up high on the roof."

We joined the crowd getting into an elevator, and no one commented when I pushed the "R" button.

*　*　*

The winds on the hospital's rooftop were just as strong as ever, and I was eager to let them lift me skyward. The shed for the elevator mechanism, the water tank, and some other machinery occupied the left side of the roof, leaving the right flat and unobstructed. I hurried over to the empty space.

Winnie watched intently as I drew the fingers of my right hand horizontally through the air while I swept the fingers of my left hand vertically, as if I was weaving fabric. I reversed the motions, as if I was unweaving it, and then repeated the first motion, as if I was weaving a new pattern. At the same time, I murmured the spell, and the world swam in a golden haze. The next moment, my human form and clothing had disappeared and I was my proper shape again. I picked up the purse full of pearls and placed the strap around my neck.

Winnie started to put out her hand but hesitated. "Can I touch you?"

"If you must," I said.

I craned my neck over to watch as she brushed her palm over my scales and then traced the edges of one. "They're so smooth," she marveled. "And they shine like jewels. I think you look nicer when you're yourself."

"So do I," I said. "If you'd been this respectful the first time we met, you would have gotten off on a better paw with me."

"I was sort of disappointed in your den, not you." She waved her hand over her head. "Maybe it's how the sun makes you gleam now."

"*Humph,* yes, it's all in the lighting." I suspected there was more to it than that: Winnie was careful to hide her true feelings when meeting someone for the first time. Now that she felt more comfortable with me, she was showing what she really felt. *Well, you haven't seen anything yet.* Crouching, I said, "Hop on."

When she clambered up between my wings, I twisted my long neck around and saw that her hands had clasped two of my scales. "Squeeze your legs tighter against me."

"I know how to ride," she answered. "But I've never ridden bareback before."

I could have told her that riding a dragon was going to be quite different from riding a horse. But I knew she would find out soon enough. I stood still so she could find her balance on my back, settle in, and grip my sides as well as she could.

When she had done so, I raised a foreleg and turned in a slow circle, as if I was drawing a curtain around us, at the same time that my claws drew the signs.

"What are you doing?" she asked.

It's just as well that I have such excellent powers of concentration because I finished the spell flawlessly. "... *antartis!*"

It was only then that I twisted my neck so I could stare directly into her eyes. "Never, never interrupt me when I'm casting a spell. Some of them have dire consequences if you make a mistake or stop in the middle."

She swallowed, but even now her fear couldn't overcome her curiosity. "What would happen?"

"We could turn inside out," I snapped, "or worse."

Her eyes grew big. "Worse?"

I turned my head so I faced the edge of the roof. "Real magic has consequences. If I make a mistake, I can't undo it by pressing a button like on a video game and returning to an earlier stage. Instead, you might never be able to speak again, and then you'd explode because you couldn't pester me with any more questions."

"Ha! I'd write my questions instead." She was a plucky little thing.

"Undoubtedly," I said. "As it happens, I was casting a spell so only magicals could see us."

Then, with a majestic leap, I sprang into the air and unfurled my wings. I'd lost interest in flying when Fluffy was ill, so it was invigorating to feel the wind lift me on invisible hands.

Behind me, Winnie let out a whoop. I wasn't surprised

by her reaction. Taking a pet flying for the first time always reminds me how wonderful it is to be free in the air.

As I glided above a nearby house, the wind from our passage panicked a line of pigeons perched on the roof, and they flapped their wings in a noisy, frantic escape. High above me, I saw the white contrails of a jet plane, and in the first rush of exultation, I thought of soaring upward and circling round and round it.

But I caught myself in time because, as excellent a flier as I am, I might have accidentally bumped the plane. Thanks to the spell, though, I was free to play in the air currents, jumping from one to another like a dolphin leaping in the ocean. The currents carried me in the direction of Clipper's Emporium. She must have been feeling medieval because her cloud rose in cottony spires and battlements. Finer bits of mist whipped about like banners. Though it looked as soft and wispy as any cloud, her store was as secure and sturdy as magic could make it.

We'd arrived too soon for my taste, and I almost went on, but then I remembered I had a pet on my back. "Do you want to fly some more or shop?" I asked as I craned my head behind me.

The winds this high were biting today, but I was dressed in scales and not thin cloth. Winnie's teeth were chattering from the cold. "I th-think I'd l-like to sh-shop."

I scolded myself for not dressing her properly for the chilly higher altitudes. Skipping any more aerobatics, I made a quick, if boring, landing. "We'd better get you inside," I said to Winnie.

When she slid off my back, she was shivering, and when she tried to walk, she lurched on stiff legs.

"Next time tell me if you're cold," I said.

She wrapped her arms around herself for greater warmth. "And give you an excuse to leave me behind?"

"Don't turn into an icicle just because you want to show me how tough you are," I scolded, and moved alongside her to shield her from the worst of the wind.

I saw an old friend, Britomart, Clipper's Mistress of Security, barring the doorway, which her massive body did very well in its chain-mail shirt. She had raised her battle-ax to her shoulder, ready to swing at the slightest provocation.

Glaring up at her were the nastiest little kobolds I'd ever had the misfortune to meet. They only reached as high as her kneecaps, and their hair was as thick and bristly as the whiskers on a pig's snout. Somehow their pipestem necks supported their large-eared heads. It was rare to see any of them in the daylight, let alone up in the

sky. Both dwarves and kobolds are underground creatures, but kobolds are to dwarves as bottom-dwelling
catfish are to trout, living and working at depths in the
earth that even dwarves regarded as dangerous because
of the shadowy creatures there.

Small as they were, the pack of them could still give
Britomart a hard time—but not with a dragon on her side.

CHAPTER FOUR

*Avoid spoiling your pet with too many treats;
however, spoiling yourself is all well and good.*

"**S**tay close to me," I murmured to Winnie. I was
grateful that she didn't argue but slipped in close
to my right shoulder.

Then I trapped the nearest kobold in my claws and
dangled him a few feet above the cloud surface. "Excuse
me, but we have business inside."

He grunted and squealed something in Low Kobold,
and the other five kobolds turned
as one to glower at me.

Pursing my lips and
aiming carefully,
I breathed

a narrow spear of fire that singed the hair off my captive's shins. The big baby screeched as if I was actually barbecuing him instead of giving him a dragon's beauty treatment.

When I dropped him, he scrambled away on all fours, and as I took a step forward, the pack of bullies shoved one another in their hurry to get out of my way.

I raised a paw to my mouth as I gave a little burp, and a wisp of smoke rose into the air. "Next time my fire will reach deeper than your hair," I warned them.

Britomart was chuckling as she bowed and then turned sideways to let me pass. As I went by her, I whispered, "Let me know if this lot gives you any more trouble."

"Aye, and thank you, Miss Drake," she said with another bow.

Just inside the doorway was a small copper pyramid. I could see the tips of scarlet claws peeking from inside. Then the two-inch-long lobster-like pemburu crawled forward to bar our way. Its segmented shell was an iridescent blue-green and its tail a brilliant scarlet too. Its eyestalks shifted the spherical gold eyes from Winnie to me, and it strained at its silver collar and leash, which were tied to the pyramid by a slender chain.

Fascinated, Winnie squatted down. "It looks like a piece of jewelry."

I put a paw on Winnie's shoulder. "Stay still." The pemburu began to glow inside, pulsing rhythmically for a moment before the light dulled. When the pemburu crept back into its home, Britomart said, "Okay, you can shop now."

"What was all that about?" Winnie asked.

"The pemburu can sniff magic," Britomart explained. "We had to get one after a shoplifting wizard tried to sneak in an enchanted sack—a truly bottomless one."

"What are things coming to?" I sympathized.

It was as warm inside as it was breezy and cold outside. A floating cloud emporium posed certain challenges in climate control, but high in the misty rafters, clusters of fluttering sapphire bats and glowing air snails worked together to keep the temperature suitable for Clipper and her customers.

At the moment, Clipper was above chilly San Francisco, but the air currents could carry her shop wherever she wanted, from the Bering Sea to Zanzibar—and her merchandise reflected it too.

Elegant and bold banners hung from misty hooks hidden from view, flooding the air above with floating trails of color. Each time I visited the Emporium, it seemed to have more and more merchandise, scattered in displays all around, and more things drifting down from the heights above. Bundles of sweetgrass might lie next to a

41

tower of artfully arranged scimitars. On one table, random jars of polishing cream were stacked neatly—one or another would brighten up tarnished armor, moldy merman scales, or a pirate captain's hook. I'd spent many an afternoon browsing and getting delightfully lost before asking for help. Yet the organization all made sense to Clipper, and she always knew where anything could be found.

"Look!" cried Winnie as a small shadow glided over our heads. "It's a little pteranodon. Wow!"

Clipper also had a small menagerie of creatures suitable as company for the lonely sorceress or as guardians for the frightened lord of a castle. They were all rare and magical—most with very limited skills, but pleasant to watch since they could change colors or do something amusing. In one cage, a fuzzy lavender lemur stared at us with eyes that seemed to cover half its face, and it opened its muzzle to trill an aria. Inside a tall glass column full of exotic plants, dream-casting moths and other rare insects drifted from blossom to blossom, and neon lizards basked on crystal branches. I've always enjoyed watching the amphibious warbling doves glide through the air and swim across their tank, their gills fluttering around their necks. Nearby, lithe Lady Jane salamanders raced around and around on wheels, and fluffy pink carousel mice spun like tops in a dome of their own.

"Oh, my dad would have loved these," Winnie said, drawn to a tower for the dragonets, each in its own separate compartment. "They're like you . . . but teeny."

"Watch your fingers," I told her quickly. "Or they'll be toasted."

I did not approve of keeping dragonets as pets. Still, Clipper treated all her little friends well and called them her guests. And she always verified that their new owners knew what they were getting into and would provide good homes.

Charmed by the aisles of beasts, Winnie would never have gone any farther, but I gently pushed her to the left, where Clipper was hovering.

Clipper was an air sprite, thin and light as a wisp of smoke, so she always seemed about to be blown away by the next breeze. Over four hundred years ago, when I had been in London with my pet Renwick, I'd introduced her to a neighbor, an actor named William. Her large eyes and delicate features had inspired him to write a funny little piece about the midsummer that still seems to please audiences today.

Looks aside, she was no pushover and a tough negotiator. I could see she was in the middle of a transaction with a customer haggling for a bargain.

"I've offered you a fair price for the carnelian," the

creature said, pointing to the stack of gold coins on the counter. He looked roughly like a human, though most of his weight was in his large hips and thick legs. He had hunched forward so the large eye on the top of his head could look at her. Even without the clan markings tattooed around the eye, I recognized him as a drought demon. His kind could turn a watery paradise into a desert, but I'd never known any to be interested in semi-precious gems.

"Not for a stone from King Solomon's ring," Clipper said. The carnelian glowed like a winter sun, deep orange with a blush of red, as it nestled on a black velvet cushion. She held a magnifying glass over it. "You can see the marks left by the worm that cut it."

Winnie started to turn her head to ask me about a gem-carving worm, but I held up a hand. My friend Clipper might be in trouble.

The drought demon didn't bother looking through the magnifying glass. "Clouds are made of water, and water can dry up, as I know all too well," he warned.

Clipper put down the magnifying glass and picked up a delicate porcelain cup. "Don't you dare threaten me on my property," she said, taking a sip of tea.

"I was just giving some friendly advice," the drought demon said. "You won't like it if I become unfriendly."

Winnie tugged at my wing anxiously. "Do something, Miss Drake," she whispered urgently.

As dainty as Clipper looked, she had not survived all these centuries without learning a trick or two. "My friend can take care of herself," I whispered back.

"The negotiations are over. Get out." Clipper's long, slender fingers fished a slice of lemon from the cup and flipped the lemon right onto the exposed eyeball of the demon.

As the creature clutched at his eye, his screech made the merchandise sway under the rafters, but he shut up when he felt my paws grip his head like a vise.

"Blink your eye rapidly, and you'll be all right," I instructed.

The eyelid fluttered up and down quickly, and when the creature could focus his eye again, I made sure he got a close-up view of me and my fangs. "I think you left some kobold trash outside. I suggest you take them and yourself away from here and never come back."

With a gulp, the creature sidled around me and scurried down the aisle. Britomart heard him coming and stepped aside so he could hurry past her.

"A drought demon with a gang of kobolds." Clipper sighed. "San Francisco never ceases to amaze me."

"The whole world comes here," I sympathized, "and

unfortunately that includes the scum. Have they been giving you a lot of trouble?'"

"This is the first time I've seen them, and I hope it's the last." Clipper set her cup down. "But I'm glad to see you. I was so sorry to hear about—"

"Amelia?" I said before she could say "Fluffy." "Yes, many people were." I put a paw on Winnie's shoulder. "This is her great-niece, Winnie."

"Winnie, WIN-nie, win-NIE." Clipper chewed the syllables as if testing them for flavor. Then she shook her head. "I think you can find a better name for her than that."

"What does she mean?" Winnie asked.

"Just a little sprite humor," I said with a warning look at Clipper. "Do you have a pound of my usual tea?'"

"I just got in a new shipment," Clipper said. "And as thanks for helping me, I'll throw in some of those seaweed cakes you like so much." She arched an eyebrow. "Or perhaps you'd prefer a tiara for the Spelling Bee."

Winnie immediately piped up. "You get a crown for spelling words?"

I held a claw up to my muzzle. "You're not supposed to interrupt grown-ups when they're holding a conversation."

Clipper leaned forward and said in a conspiratorial

46

voice to Winnie, "She's always cranky before she's had her afternoon tea."

Winnie tilted forward so she could whisper loudly, "Do you have anything else that will make a dragon less grumpy?"

Clipper folded her arms in amusement. "Short of a personality transplant, no. But I do have a nice selection of wooden clubs. Perhaps one of them would do the trick."

I tapped Winnie's snout. "I didn't bring you here just so you could insult me."

She looked right past my claw and at Clipper. "I'll take the biggest club you have."

"I'm afraid you don't look strong enough to lift it." Resting her arms on the counter, Clipper smiled. "But I can tell you what the Spelling Bee is, since the old grump won't." As an old friend enjoying this new game, Clipper ignored my frantic signals to keep quiet.

Winnie listened with growing excitement as Clipper told her about tomorrow's Enchanters' Fair. "All the magical creatures get together and hold all sorts of competitions. And at the end, there's a contest of wits and spells that we call the Spelling Bee, and the winner becomes the monarch of the festival." Clipper motioned to me. "Miss Drake has won every year since it started."

"I'm going to let someone else be Queen Bee this year," I said impatiently. Lowering my head, I slid my purse off my neck and emptied the pearls into a nearby tray. "Please deduct my purchases from this and transfer the remaining money to the usual account." That was the trust fund that Whitlock, Hound and Spurge administered. They would draw from the fund to pay Winnie's tuition to the Spriggs Academy. It offered its students a range of unique educational opportunities, but none of them came cheap.

"Certainly," Clipper said, beginning to count the shining pearls. "You've been very busy, Miss Drake." Her delicate eyebrows immediately rose. "Ah, of course, you've been grieving for Miss Amelia." She nodded sympathetically as she finally understood why I had so many pearls and why I didn't feel like participating in the Spelling Bee.

Winnie, though, couldn't get the Fair out of her head. "I think you ought to enter the contest this year."

"You have no say in this," I said firmly, and added to Clipper, "Winnie needs something lightweight but warm when we fly."

"I have just the thing." Clipper drifted up into the misty heights and then descended with a silvery scarf. "This is woven from the wool of ice sheep."

"Ice sheep?" Winnie asked.

Clipper wound the scarf around Winnie's neck until the lower half of her face was hidden by woolen folds. "There. You'll be nice and toasty-roasty in a moment."

I thought of Winnie's painting. She had promise as an artist, but of course, it would never do to praise a pet unduly. Their heads can swell up with the tiniest crumb of flattery. "And something to keep Winnie from becoming idle before school starts. Perhaps a sketchbook to draw in?"

From under the counter, Clipper drew a sketchbook covered in crimson shantung silk. "I've got something every other artist will envy. I found this in an old trunk that I bought at an auction. The pages are all empty, and I'll sell it half price for my new friend."

Winnie caressed the silk cover and mumbled something about its smoothness.

Suddenly she yanked the scarf away from her mouth. "Hey, it tingles."

"That's probably static electricity from the silk on the cover," I said.

"Or residual magic from my shop." Clipper began to wrap my purchases in blue paper and tie up the bundle neatly with red twine.

If my friend had only known what the sketchbook really was, she would never have parted with it for a roomful of dragon pearls but kept it for herself. And if I had known how much trouble it was going to cause, I would never have let Winnie touch it—let alone use it.

CHAPTER FIVE

*Encourage your pet to pursue his or her talents
or your pet will be bored and bore you as well.*

The scarf kept Winnie comfortable on the flight
back, just as Clipper had promised. But I should
have tied it around her mouth like a gag. All the way
home, she kept pestering me about the Fair, especially
the Spelling Bee.

I landed on the hospital rooftop and transformed

to my human form, and we walked back to my rooms, where I was looking forward to curling up with a well-earned cup of tea. Winnie, though, began to poke and pry around my living room. "Where's all your tiaras from the other Fairs?"

Some humans become greedy monsters when they see gold and jewels, so I didn't want to expose her to them until I knew her better.

"There are no tiaras," I fibbed. "Nor medals nor trophies nor plaques. The winner just gets some applause, and then everyone goes home."

"But Clipper said—" she began to protest.

I cut her off. "That was just more bad sprite humor."

"I think you ought to at least get a blue ribbon," Winnie said, exasperated.

"Like a prize cow? No thank you," I said. "The real prize is the satisfaction of being the best in San Francisco."

"And beating everyone else," Winnie grunted.

I thought of my rival, Silana, grinding her teeth year after year when I won, and I simply smiled. But when Winnie kicked off her shoes and flopped down on my sofa as if she were trying to put a permanent dent in it, I tried to hint that she should leave. "Don't you have to go and check on your mother?"

"Nope." Winnie showed me her smartphone. "Mom texted me that the therapist said she's doing really well and that she's meeting Ms. Dylis for tea."

Dylis Whitlock was the lawyer who handled the trust. She came from a fine old dwarf family and had her ear to the stone, as the dwarves liked to say when they thought someone was sensible. I was glad that she and Winnie's mother had hit it off—just not this afternoon.

Winnie pillowed her head on her hands. "You know, I wouldn't mind having some tea myself."

I pretended to yawn. "Actually, I was thinking of taking a nap."

The second hint sailed over her head just like the first one had. "Go ahead. I'll make my own tea." She swung her legs off the sofa.

I could have retreated into my bedroom for some privacy and a rest, but leaving Winnie unsupervised in my living room was like asking a cat to babysit a nest of chicks. Nothing would be the same when I returned.

"Perhaps I'm feeling a little parched after all," I said, and changed to my proper form. "Ah, much more comfortable." I stretched luxuriously.

She knew enough now not to interrupt me in mid-spell. "What's *kloot . . . kloot . . .* ?" she asked.

So she'd been watching and listening. *"Kluttänk,"*

I corrected her. "It means 'change' in a language long dead." And just in case she had any ideas of trying to change her own shape, I added, "But you'll get frustrated if you try to copy me. You have to put a bit of your soul into a spell before it'll work. It's like putting fuel into the gas tank of a car."

"Teach me," she said eagerly.

"It's not my place to do that," I told her, "and very few can work magic, so don't be disappointed if you can't."

Fluffy was not magically inclined, but managed, with a little help, to pass her introductory classes at Spriggs. She learned about magic in them yet never was able to pursue it further. She didn't need to. She had me to protect her. And so would Winnie.

"Will you please open the parcel and get the tea?" I asked.

As she tore off the paper excitedly, I thought her face must look as happy as this when she opened a birthday present—whether it had been bought in a store or was a homemade one like her checkers. She never took her eyes off the silk sketchbook as she handed me the tea.

When I brought the tray of tea things from the kitchen, Winnie was lying on her stomach, drawing in her new sketchbook. She was focused on her work, filling page after page.

As I set the seaweed cakes on a platter and prepared the tea, I glanced at her every now and then. If Winnie had been a cat, I think she would have been purring contentedly.

Sitting down in my favorite chair, I found myself enjoying the scene after all. I was glad that Winnie had insisted on staying.

I leaned my head back and began to see the possibilities the future might hold for us, my new pet and me. I couldn't imagine a cozier picture than Winnie drawing on the sofa while I sipped my tea. And I wondered if Fluffy had known how much Winnie would need a friend—and that I would need one too.

Maybe she expected our lives together to be like this . . . full of happy flights and quiet, pleasant moments.

If so, how very wrong she was.

Later that evening, as Winnie slumbered in her bedroom and I fell asleep in my apartment, our dreams were sweet and forgettable. But in the cool, foggy summer night, something was stirring—something unpredictable and unforgettable.

I did not know what was happening then, but I can imagine it now.

The sketchbook sitting by Winnie's open window began to glow, a pale shimmer first dancing along the edges and then spreading across the covers and down the spine. Then the pages inside began to gleam from one to the next until all were shining with a golden light.

The pages fluttered, gently, then wilder and wilder, until the book was flung open, the dancing pages flickering and fanning in a half circle of light. Quickly, small, frightened shapes skittered into the darkness: some leaping to the floor below, some fleeing and fluttering out the window, down the ivy vines, and into the misty garden.

Magic seen can be thrilling or horrifying. But too often unseen magic simply changes the way things are in bewildering ways.

Before dawn, the book snapped shut, dark and still again, and all our troubles began.

CHAPTER SIX

～◦～◦～

*Be firm with your pet and make it clear what
is acceptable behavior. Both you and your pet
will be happier for it.*

E arly Saturday morning, I had resolved to curl up
with a good book and stay in my apartment all day.

I made a pot of Rangoon tea, but as the flowery scent
filled the living room, I heard the rapping at the door.

Winnie's voice sounded muffled from beyond. "Miss
Drake, you gotta see this."

"Civilized conversation begins only after my first cup
of tea," I answered loudly. "So go away."

I heard Winnie's key click in the
lock.

Be firm, I told myself, *no matter
how much she cries or begs to stay.*

"Look, I have something to show you." Winnie sailed triumphantly into the room, balancing her sketchbook on her palms as if she were presenting a huge diamond. She twirled around and around and laid it on the coffee table. "Come see. Come see," she called merrily.

What I could see was one silly little flibbertigibbet who was not going to be satisfied until I did what she asked.

"I spent all evening working on it," she said, flopping on the couch. "I used all the colored pencils I could find to make everything look right." Picking up the book, she spread it open wide so I couldn't miss the display.

"Well," I said, folding my forelegs, "I've heard of invisible ink before, but not invisible pencils."

The sketchbook's pages were blank—as blank as they were when Clipper sold it to us.

Winnie's head dipped down to look.

"They're gone," she said in dismay, and began to flip through page after page. "Every single one is gone."

I was just about to say something witty and perhaps a bit sharp, but when I saw how upset she was, I bit my tongue.

"What is gone?" I asked her as softly as I could. As she stared at a blank page, she was growing more distressed by the moment. So I slipped the book from her grasp and shut it with a *thud*.

"My pictures." Winnie's voice was trembling. "My wonderful, wonderful pictures of the rare and magical creatures. But now they're all gone. What *happened*?"

As my paws held the book, I felt a thin but lingering tingle run across my claws. Dread slid like a small, swift lizard down my shoulders, settling between my wings.

I shivered. *Oh, Clipper. There was magic in this book. Why didn't you sense it? Why didn't I? Or did something awaken the magic just now?* It felt like a restless kind of magic, too, one that wanted to be noticed.

With her tiny snout, Winnie would have missed the many clues that a dragon could detect. Lifting the book, I sniffed it cautiously and smelled the graphite, wax, and pigments of her modern pencils. They almost masked the scent of papyrus reeds harvested from a marsh under a full moon . . . the dampness of silkworms weaving their cocoons upon a golden skeleton . . . and the . . . yes—it was unmistakable—the bark from the dancing trees of Serendip, which dance only in a solar eclipse.

Paper is made partly with linen or other plant fibers, but only a strange and magical paper would be made with such exotic and costly ingredients.

I was the one who needed calming now, so I took several deep breaths before I picked up my tablet. As she began to thumb through her sketchbook again, looking for her missing pictures, I searched the magical databases. I didn't like what I found.

"Winnie, did you remove the book's seal?" I asked.

She drew her eyebrows together in puzzlement. "You mean like the kind with flippers that eats fish?"

"No, the seal could have been some symbol drawn inside the book, or perhaps a piece of wax with a design stamped on it—or even something like a sticker," I explained.

"Well, there was something," Winnie said. "A bunch of squiggly lines that suddenly showed up inside the back cover. I thought some kid had scribbled them there, but they came right off when I rubbed them." She held up her thumb.

"That would have been the seal," I said, feeling the wing muscles tense tightly along my shoulders. So much for my leisurely day of reading. "And it probably only appeared to the book's owner at a certain hour each night. Removing the seal let your sketchlings come to life. They're currently wandering around the neighborhood and perhaps all around San Francisco."

"Cool," Winnie said.

It was not quite the reaction I had been expecting. Fear or remorse or confusion, yes, but not such . . . enthusiasm.

"No, it is not cool," I corrected her. "Remember what I told you about the Agreement?"

"Sure, but I haven't told anyone about you or the other magicals," she said.

"According to the Agreement," I explained, "we magicals cannot use our powers or work magic openly where too many humans can find out."

Winnie asked, "Like if some of the neighbors saw my sketchlings . . . ?"

"It would be bad," I said. "So let's not let things come to that." I got another cup from the kitchen and poured tea into it. Then I placed it in front of Winnie. "While you drink this, I want you to try to remember how many pictures you drew."

Winnie took a sip. "Umpteen."

I told myself to be patient. "Umpteen is not as precise a figure as I would like."

Winnie stared into her cup a moment. "I drew something different across each page. I think I filled at least a quarter of the sketchbook."

I flicked open the book and fanned the pages. "I count eighty pages, and if you were right about a quarter full, we should have twenty to find."

"How did you count the pages so fast?" Winnie asked.

"Training," I told her. "Some skills are no longer

taught or valued. A shame. But back to the sketchbook. Did you draw a kobold or drought demon?"

She seemed offended. "Why would I want to draw those wicked and mean things? I like interesting things and pretty ones—like that pemburu. I got to use so many colored pencils when I drew it. I added a few new colors for fun."

The pemburu had been so small that I didn't worry about it. "What else?"

She sipped her tea and thought for a bit. "There was that mini-pteranodon."

"Not pretty, but interesting." Picking up my tablet, I carefully tapped the buttons on the reinforced screen.

"Yup," said Winnie. "I saw a big one at the natural history museum. My dad took me there whenever he could. We both loved the dinosaur rooms the most."

To her credit and my dismay, Winnie had a remarkable memory of many of the magical creatures she had seen in Clipper's shop. Some she had drawn just one sketch of, and others she drew several times. So there were two dragonets and a couple of neon lizards to track down. Delightful!

I counted the list. "That makes nineteen. What about number twenty?"

Winnie shifted uneasily and looked away. "Maybe that was all."

Pandora and her box, I muttered to myself, *had nothing on you and your sketchbook, my pet.* But I could see she was feeling bad about the runaway sketches, so I memorized the list. When I finished, I set the tablet on the coffee table. "Well, our day is planned. We're going on a Beast Hunt before too many people see your sketchlings and we violate the Agreement. Once we've returned all the creatures to the book, we'll re-seal it if I can't think of something better to do with them."

"Where do we start?" Winnie asked.

"Perhaps you should check your room first," I advised her. "There might be a straggler or two. And if we're very lucky, we'll be done by lunchtime."

I was mentally crossing my claws on that promise when I heard a noise from outside. Had Winnie's mother followed her down here? Hurrying to the door, I opened it and poked my head outside. I thought I glimpsed a long shadow disappearing behind a stack of shipping crates.

Winnie peeked through the doorway. "What's wrong?"

"I thought I heard something." I tested the air, but I could smell only myself and Winnie—and the dust.

"Do you think it was one of the sketchlings?" Winnie asked.

Perhaps the long shadow had just been a trick of the light. "Yes, and it must be so small that I can't find its scent," I said. I trusted my snout more than I did my eyes, so I dismissed my suspicions—and made things even worse.

CHAPTER SEVEN

~~~∾⌒∾~~~

A hunt is good exercise for both you and your pet.

As soon as Winnie left, I used my tablet to go to the special website that only a few magicals knew and began reading the *Thaumaturgica Chaldea*, a Latin translation of spells from the famous wizards of ancient Babylonia. The scanned parchment was worn thin, with the spidery characters showing through from the other side. But with my sharp dragon eyes, I quickly found the chapter "Capturing and Containing," then the section "Creatures Large and Small," and finally the subheading "Willing and Recalcitrant."

The enchantment was quick, efficient, and workmanlike—as you would expect for wizards capturing monsters and demons. Make a spell too complicated and you'll be eaten or blasted before you can complete it. This one should be more than sufficient for the sketchlings—even so, I sincerely hoped that we wouldn't find many escapees too large and too recalcitrant.

I practiced sketching the word *šuti,* which meant "catch" or "seize" in Sumerian. My claws found it easy to scratch the cuneiform syllables in the air. Then I drew an eight-pointed star around it with my left paw and a triangular arrowhead with my right. I finished by dragging the arrowhead through the star. At the same time, I rehearsed the brief chant in a soft mutter that the *Thaumaturgica* had translated into Latin—*Te Superi dabunt mihi* for one creature and *Vos Superi dabunt mihi* for two or more.

I had it down by the time Winnie arrived with a glowing snail, which had crept under her bed, and two small neon lizards all tangled in a butterfly net. "I found the pair trying to eat the watercolors in my paint box."

"How colorful," I said. When I examined them, I

could see why the lizards hadn't left. . . . Winnie had spent more time capturing their brilliant shades of orange and pink than drawing their feet. They were small stumps, not suited for climbing, scurrying, or even walking very far.

I began the ancient enchantment. "Please hold the book for me. I need my paws free to sign the spell."

Winnie held the net in one hand while her other began to open the sketchbook to a blank page.

Up until now the sketchlings had been docile, but suddenly they frantically began to climb out of the net. Of course, the snail couldn't go very fast or far, but through the net's mesh, I could see its footpad rippling and its eyestalks straining as it tried to creep up the net.

The lizards, though, might have scooted away, but before they could, Winnie dropped the sketchbook and grabbed the mesh near the net's opening and squeezed it shut.

They hunched, their bodies pulsing with waves of color, tails lifted like flagpoles, as they hissed and snapped at us.

"The ones at Clipper's were so quiet," Winnie said. "What's gotten into these?"

"They seem scared of returning to the sketchbook," I said.

Winnie felt sorry for them. "Maybe they just want to

be free. Would it be all right if I kept them in an aquarium tank?"

I chopped my paw through the air. "We can't take the risk. It would still violate the Agreement if your mother or some visitor saw them in your room."

"Okay," she said sadly. Holding the net shut, she got the sketchbook in her other hand and clumsily spread it open.

Making the signs with my paws, I murmured the magical words. The next instant, the book became a magnet, drawing the snail and lizards with a zipping noise through the air and onto the pages, where they became two-dimensional drawings once again.

Winnie slapped the book shut. "Well, that's three down—now for the rest." She picked up a sturdy lace shoulder bag from the back of a chair. "Can I use this to carry my book?"

"Be my guest." I reviewed her list in my memory. "A sapphire bat is nocturnal, so it probably couldn't have gotten very far before sunrise." I tapped a claw against my snout. "If I were it, I'd want someplace dark and quiet. And I didn't smell it in the basement."

"Then how about the garage?" suggested Winnie.

"Is your mother at home?" I asked.

"Don't worry," Winnie said. "Mom left to run some

easy errands, and she said she'd be gone the whole day."

"I'd still better change first," I said. "We might have to leave the house and grounds."

"Why don't you just use those spells so people don't see you?" Winnie asked.

I shook my head. "That's fine when I'm in the air, but on the ground, you don't need to see me to know I'm there. I might be invisible, but people could see the grass flatten as I walk by."

The world shimmered in a golden haze as I transformed. But today, my hair was red and artfully curled over my forehead.

Winnie circled me. "I like the hair, and you look like you just stepped out of a fashion magazine."

I smoothed my lime-green sweater and picked a bit of lint from my navy skirt. "I take pride in my disguises, so I keep up on the latest human fripperies." I had digital subscriptions to all the fashion magazines, and many of the top houses put the highlights of their new season's clothes online.

We left through my front door, slipping around the furniture in the storage room that hid my apartment. The rest of the basement was just as cluttered, except for the area around the furnace.

It was quiet on the first floor. The staff had been given time off because Dylis, the lawyer who managed the trust, had not been sure when Liza and Winnie would arrive.

I smiled seeing all of the portraits and landscapes decorating the hallway walls. Winthrop had called them his windows on the world, and he'd bought them during our later travels. He had wanted to see and do so much, but as with all my pets, his human body had been no match for his great energy and will. Despite all their claims otherwise, humans are such fragile creatures.

This was no time for sentimentality, though. Magic, uncontrolled and unpredictable, was loose and possibly wreaking havoc around us. Recapturing the runaway sketchlings should be my only concern right now, and I had just started to look around for them when a woman in her late thirties limped in from the kitchen. She was wearing jeans and a white pullover sweater, and her hair was as frizzy as Winnie's.

The woman gave a startled cry when she saw us. "Oh!"

But then she shocked *us* when she went on to say, "Oh, it's you, Miss Drake. I was hoping to meet you sometime."

Winnie and I glanced at each other, and she was the first to recover.

"Mom, Miss Drake was a friend of Great-Aunt Amelia."

"Oh, I know all about our guest, Win," she said, extending her hand to me. "I'm Liza, and my aunt told me about you, Miss Drake."

Oh, Fluffy, what secrets did you reveal?

Her grip was firm and strong, her palm callused from hard work, her cheeks brown and rough from too much wind, rain, and sun. Yes, this outdoorsy girl would have bewildered her father, Jarvis, who preferred sitting in a chair as much as possible.

"Hello," I said pleasantly. "I've been meaning to see how you were settling in, but Winnie told me you had other plans today."

"I forgot my cell phone. But what nice luck to have a chance to meet you now. I was so sorry we weren't able to be here in time for Aunt Amelia's funeral and greet all her friends." She picked up her phone and clicked through her pictures. "Here is a photo that Aunt Amelia scanned and sent me not long ago."

I saw our smiling faces and smiled back, admiring again her soft, wavy hair. Its lushness had prompted my name of endearment for her. I could read Fluffy's tidy penmanship on the bottom:

Miss Drake and me

"I sensed you were a good friend," Liza said with a smile.

"Yes, we were," I said. "And I promised her I would watch over the two of you."

"Wonderful," she said. "Aunt Amelia's lawyer has been such a big help already. She's arranged for Winnie to attend the Spriggs Academy, where Aunt Amelia studied."

"I'm glad to hear the Academy had the good sense to accept Winnie," I said truthfully. "She'll get a wonderful education there."

Liza nodded. "Anyway, let's have lunch soon. I'd love to get to know you better."

"Yes, let's," I said, intending to do just the opposite.

Liza seemed to think I was a fellow natural, so since Fluffy had been cautious about revealing my true identity to her, so would I. Instead, I'd shrink to fly-size and observe Liza until I could decide if she shared the same virtues as her daughter.

As Liza limped through the front door, I thought, *In the meantime, my dear lady, we have to keep you too occupied to think about me. Perhaps a job . . . maybe something horsey.* I would deal with that problem after we snared the sketchlings.

Winnie would have gone to the garage immediately,

but I held up a hand until I heard a car back out of the driveway into the street.

"I was wondering," Winnie said, "who took that picture of you and Great-Aunt Amelia?"

"My friend Reynard," I said. "He was very fond of Fl—your great-aunt. Leave it to him to *take* a picture, not *be* in one. He's not someone who likes to be caught in anything, even a photo."

"When will I meet him?" she asked.

"Only when and if he wants you to," I told her, and walked ahead into the garage.

I put a finger on my lips, and we let our eyes adjust to the gloom before we began to look around. A few minutes later, Winnie tapped my arm and pointed. I glimpsed the brilliant blue among the row of rakes and brooms.

We moved quietly until we were next to it. I motioned to myself and then pantomimed that I would expose the bat. I wasn't sure Winnie would understand, so I was grateful when she nodded and drew the sketchbook from the lace bag.

I gently lifted a rake away to reveal the delicate blue bat hanging upside down from a shelf and sound asleep. With its wings folded around it, it looked like a sapphire carving.

Winnie opened the book, but the moment the bat

heard the rustling pages, its eyes snapped open. Its nostrils flared. Its jaws stretched, revealing needle-sharp teeth. Like any cornered animal, the bat was ready to fight. It launched itself from the wall straight at Winnie.

Grabbing her, I snatched her clear from danger and ducked my own head. The bat flapped past us and on across the garage to throw itself against the single small window on the wall. Its wings beat a frantic tapping tattoo against the glass.

One spell from me, one flick of the book from Winnie, and it was caught before it could hurt itself.

Puzzled, I studied the picture of the terrified creature. "Sapphire bats are usually so calm."

"It must really hate the sketchbook too," Winnie said guiltily.

As we went back into the house, Winnie headed for a hall closet. "Let's check in here." She rooted around among the coats hanging on the pole and then put a finger to her lips and pointed at a rain boot.

I peeked at the sleepy carousel-spinning mouse curled up inside. Like the bat, it woke the moment it heard the sketchbook opening. It leapt from the boot and became a blur as it raced from the closet and down the hallway carpet. Winnie flung herself after it, catching it more by luck than skill.

"You've got a talent for thinking like a sketchling," I said.

Though she was pleased, she gave a shrug. "I drew them after all."

I must say that I was delighted at how quickly we were catching the sketchlings because of her. So after checking the rooms in the house, I left the decision to Winnie. "Where should we look next?"

"You're asking me?" she said in surprise. But as she thought, her eyes fastened on a window. The greenness of the lawn seemed to pull at her. "Let's try the garden."

CHAPTER EIGHT

*You may know best—but sometimes
your pet may be right.*

Sure enough, we found
a slender Lady Jane
salamander sunning itself
in the birdbath. It was still
as a statue, but as soon as
Winnie opened the book,
it skittered from the bowl
and down the pedestal.

We were racing over the
gravel after it when it suddenly
stopped, sides moving in and out
slowly. As we neared it, though, I

suddenly felt sleepy. Winnie began yawning continuously.

Even though I could see a perfectly normal path in front of me, I had a strong feeling that I was going to fall into a dark pit where something was waiting to devour me. Next to me, Winnie had started to tremble as if she, too, was experiencing something frightful.

I forced my groggy mind to remember the list, then glanced at the garden lamp, where three dream-casting moths had woken from their daytime slumber and were working their magic by waving their wings rhythmically. "Book," I said.

Winnie was stiff with fear, but showing her true mettle, she managed to get the sketchbook open.

My hands and mouth moved sluggishly, as if I was in a living nightmare, but we put the salamander back into the sketchbook. And the sleepiness and fear vanished the instant the moths were returned to their pages.

Winnie gave her head a little shake. "It was almost like the salamander was leading us into an ambush."

"Except it got caught itself." I gazed at the pages. "I've never heard of dream casters being so strong before. For their magic to have such force, they must have tapped into their own personal fears."

Winnie closed the book and put it away. "But why would they think we were going to eat them?"

"Or perhaps it was something else in the book," I said.

"Maybe the pemburu?" Winnie asked. "Those claws would scare me if I was their size."

"I suppose it will still be a threat once we capture it and will remain that until we can reseal the book," I said.

"We could put lots of blank pages between the pemburu and the other sketchlings," Winnie suggested.

"Hmm, you mean isolate it? Yes, that might work." I tapped a finger against my chin. "But the sketchlings won't know our plan to keep them safe. They associate the book with the pemburu now, even though it's gone, and they'll do everything to avoid it." I shrugged. "But it can't be helped. So . . . ?" I waved a palm at her for her to decide where to search.

Knowing that I trusted her, Winnie grinned as she began to think. "Hmm." At that moment, her stomach growled, and I recalled that we hadn't had breakfast yet. She pressed a hand against her belly. "If I'm hungry, the sketchlings must be too. But what would they eat?"

I reviewed her list in my mind. "There are a bunch of vegetarians." So we scoured the garden. Fortunately the roses were in full bloom, and this year not even the foggy summer had prevented a luscious display of blossoms.

"Even magical creatures are drawn to the showy," I

said as we hunted about the dazzling red and pink and yellow and white flowers.

We found three flying insects there, fairy sirens. We were lucky that the roses had captivated them before they could scatter throughout the city.

With one bold sweep, Winnie snagged them in her net. "I don't think this one would have gone far." She pointed at a spoonlike bug with lopsided wings. "I need to pay more attention to legs and wings, I can see that."

"A good lesson," I told her, "but one I'm grateful you are learning now and not yesterday."

I knew nothing about the insects other than their name, but they were so small I didn't think they would give us any trouble.

But they didn't wait for Winnie to open the sketchbook. As soon as they saw the cover, I felt their terror. They began to make a rasping noise like a saw cutting an iron nail, and small dots rose from the garden into the air, becoming ribbons that darted toward us. As they drew near, I saw they were gnats, ladybugs, bees, wasps, and small biting flies the size of rice grains. I hadn't realized the garden was teeming with so much life, and summoned by the fairy sirens, it had now become an angry insect armada bearing down on us.

I had no idea that such small things could be so dangerous. There was no way to shield Winnie with my body because there were several swarms coming at us from different directions. I only had time to ask, "Are you allergic to bees or wasps?"

And then they were on us.

"I'll be okay. Do the spell," Winnie said. "Ow!" She flinched as a bee stung her, but she resolutely kept hold of the net while her other hand flipped open the book.

The buzzing cloud of bugs that surrounded me became so thick that I couldn't see my own hands—let alone Winnie—as I made the passes. And every time I opened my mouth, some creature flew into it. I was finding it hard to breathe, yet I managed to say the spell. I could only hope Winnie had kept the sketchbook open.

Suddenly the insect swarm scattered as quickly as it had formed, and I saw my dear pet standing like a brave soldier at her post. Despite our ordeal, she'd held the sketchbook with its pages spread out, and there were the fairy sirens.

Besides being clever and courageous, she was a tough little thing. It's funny how a life of trouble can make some creatures scared of their own shadow and others— like Winnie—stronger and better. It felt good to know I could depend on her when things got difficult.

I spit out a ladybug, which wandered soggily off. "I can see some of these creatures may be a bit challenging. Are you all right?"

"Just a bee sting. I'll put some lotion on it later." Despite her wound, she was already turning in a slow circle, searching for the next sketchling. "There's one!"

She pointed to a lemon tree. Not many lemons this year, but there was a lavender lemur searching high up in the branches. Its already-large eyes grew even bigger when it saw us, and the next moment, the leaves hid it like a green curtain.

"We can't catch it if the book can't see it," I whispered. "So look in the bag for some fruit."

Laying the net on the ground, Winnie rummaged through the lace bag and found a big box of raisins.

"Got it," she said softly, and tossed a few raisins on the driveway.

The lemur poked its head through the screen of leaves and sniffed the air. Catching the scent of the raisins, it glanced down at them. In the end, hunger won out over fear.

The lemur leapt from the tree and approached warily. Winnie tossed a few more raisins. The lemur stared at them and then at her, all the while singing a complicated little tune. With a run and a pounce, it went not to the raisins but to Winnie, climbing up her leg. Even as her eyebrows began to rise in surprise, the lemur's small leathery black paw grabbed the whole box from her hand.

"Hey, you!" Winnie cried in surprise. "Stop, thief!"

The furry felon had hopped to the ground and was already dashing beyond her reach, back up the tree, where it sat on a low branch and busily started gobbling up raisins.

"The book!" I said as I began the spell.

Winnie snatched the book and got into position.

Frightened, the lemur began to scrabble higher toward the cover of the leaves. Fortunately one forepaw was holding the box, so it couldn't climb as fast, and I finished the enchantment just in time.

The lemur was zapped back into the book, where the greedy little crook was captured on the page with its mouth full.

"Glad we stopped that clever one before it ate its way through San Francisco," I said.

"It's so much bigger than the pemburu, though," Winnie said. "Why was it scared?"

"Maybe it picked up the fear from the smaller sketch-lings," I suggested.

"Well, how many do we have now?" asked Winnie.

"Thirteen," I told her, "and I see another in the bottlebrush." I pointed at an amphibious warbling dove. Its drab speckled feathers told me it was a female.

"I'd better stay out of its sight till the last second,"

Winnie said, slipping behind me. As I started to murmur the words and move my hands and fingers in the mystic signs, I heard her flipping the pages of the sketchbook until she found a blank one.

It was amazing how quickly we were meshing as a team. By now, she could recognize when I was nearing the end of the spell, and she moved beside me with the pages spread. The next instant, the bird zipped from the bush into the book.

"There should be a pair," Winnie said. "A male and female."

"This is all that's left of the male." I picked up a pile of brilliant orange and blue feathers. "Those doves mate for life. I'm afraid our little sketchling is going to be alone from now on."

"A dove is too big for a pemburu to eat," Winnie said sadly. "It must've been a cat."

Taking a break from all the excitement of the chase, I sensed something that perhaps I had been too busy to notice before. I had a strong feeling that we were being watched—almost as if we were not the hunters but being hunted instead.

When a large shrub shook, Winnie aimed the book at it. "It's a sketchling—maybe the pemburu!"

I felt the breeze against my cheek as I tested the air.

I smelled only the usual scents. "The pemburu's much too small to shake a whole bush. It's just the wind."

If I had trusted Winnie's hunting instincts instead of my snout, I could have saved us so much grief later. But I ignored them and put us both in peril.

CHAPTER NINE

There are clever pets and unselfish pets,
but treasure most the pet who is both.

We continued to search under every bush and in every hole, but our luck seemed to have run out. Frustrated, I stopped and cleared my head. "Oh, how foolish. We've been thinking like groundlings and looking down rather than up. You should find some binoculars in that bag, Winnie."

Winnie was surprised when she pulled

out a pair of green binoculars. "They weren't in here before."

I shrugged. "Sometimes the bag forgets what it has until you remind it."

She stared at the binoculars and then at the lace bag. "Where did you ever get it?"

"From a wise and powerful woman in Belgium named Sefa Bubbles. She gave me the bag after I helped her out of a spot of trouble." I smiled when I remembered how I had to singe a few rich burghers before they saw things my way.

As Winnie slowly scanned the trees, I inspected the roof, gutters, and turrets. At the tip of the tallest turret, I saw the bright banner Winthrop had designed for our home. It was whipping back and forth in the breeze from the bay. "Well, that's reassuring. The three dragons are aloft and well," I said, satisfied.

Winnie tilted the binoculars up and squinted. "I count four."

"No, there are three dragons," I told her. "One red, one gold, and one blue. Bold dragons rampant."

"Well, I see two blue ones today," she said, passing me the binoculars.

I readjusted the binoculars for my eyes and saw the creature perched on the finial of the turret.

"That second blue one is no dragon. It's the mini-pteranodon."

"Poor thing," Winnie said, sensing the beast's loneliness. "I bet it mistook the dragons for cousins."

I clicked my tongue in annoyance. "How could you mistake a dragon's noble snout for a pteranodon's gnarly beak?"

But it did look rather sad. Perhaps it was a young one, too, looking for its mother. If it should leave here and fly about, I could see the headlines in the *Chronicle* about the sighting of an extinct flying reptile in the city. We would be in big trouble then.

"It's out of range of my capture spell," I said. "We have to draw it down to us."

Winnie rummaged around in the bag. "No more raisins."

"They wouldn't help," I said. "It eats fish."

Winnie searched through the bag. "Not even a tuna sandwich."

"That bag can be persnickety about wet and smelly items," I told her. "That's the one drawback to Sefa's creations. She likes to give them personalities as quirky as hers."

"Hmm, Dad and I always stopped to visit the pteranodon at the museum. We'd stretch our arms wide and compare them to its huge wings. He even helped teach me to read dinosaur names and the signs describing them." Winnie was squinting as if trying to see an exhibit's plaque. "Cousins to dinosaurs . . . flying reptiles . . . like birds, fly by flapping wings . . . good eyesight . . . Yes!" Suddenly she dived into the bag. "I've got to find something shiny in here."

"You'll probably feel some coins at the bottom," I said. "I always do."

Winnie dug down deep. "Got 'em." She showed me some copper coins that the Belgians of Sefa's time called double mites.

Then, using her left hand to hold the book open behind her back, she waved the coins in her right hand overhead. "Hey, hey!" she shouted until the pteranodon turned its head toward her. "Catch!" Winnie flung the double mites high in the air.

Even on such a cloudy day, the copper winked and flashed as the coins fell onto the patio.

The pteranodon launched itself from the turret, and I began the spell, but before I could finish, it settled in a palm tree, hiding among the fronds.

"Birds like shiny things," my clever pet explained. "I thought it might too. But maybe copper isn't shiny enough." She rummaged around in the purse for more coins. "Nothing," she said. "So let's try this." She undid the clasp of her medal's chain with her right hand and wound it around her fingers tightly, just in case the pteranodon was as big a thief as the lemur. Then she raised her arm and dangled the medal, letting it swing back and forth as its polished silver gleamed brightly.

The pteranodon's head moved rhythmically from side to side as if it could not take its eyes off the medal. Suddenly the flying reptile dived from the palm tree, stretching its great beak wide to snatch at it. Winnie tried to jerk the medal down, but the beast caught the disk in its beak. Instantly its mouth *clacked* shut. And twisting its head, it snapped the chain.

Winnie lunged after it desperately, the open sketchbook still in her left hand while her right hand reached for the creature. "Give that back!"

The leathery bandit was soaring beyond her reach, but not mine. I said the spell, and the next moment, the pteranodon was trapped on paper again. But there was no sign of the medal.

Winnie fell to her knees, hands probing the page for the stolen medal. "Do you think it swallowed it?" she asked, and I could sense her voice was one quiver away from a sob.

"I don't know, Winnie," I said, feeling helpless.

Perhaps losing her father's gift was like losing him all over again. "I know how much your great-grandfather's medal meant to you. I'm so sorry."

"Me too," she said, running her sleeve against her nose. Then she straightened her shoulders. "But as my dad would say, it was for a good cause."

I suppose she had learned to make sacrifices living as a fugitive from her grandfather. But this went far beyond that. She would set her grief aside so we could continue the task at hand. "Definitely," I said, appreciating her even more.

Well done, Fluffy, I praised her silently. *You made the right choice when you selected Winnie.*

I promised myself that I would find a way to make up for the lost medal somehow. But not at this moment. We were still a few creatures short of our quota.

I looked at the sun in the sky—or rather, at where it was hiding behind the clouds. "Almost time for elevenses," I said, missing my midmorning treat.

As if Sefa's bag could read my mind, I heard Winnie shout, "Look what I found inside!" She placed two bottles of ginger beer and a petite English fruitcake on a napkin. Just what two weary beast hunters needed.

"This is pretty tasty," Winnie said after breaking off chunks of cake for each of us. "I wonder how old it is."

"It's fruitcake," I said, happily munching my share. "Who could tell?"

Without a moment for adequate digestion, I saw the puffs of smoke rising from the house next door.

It was red and green angry smoke, and I knew we had to put out those fires before anyone, especially another magical, noticed.

Fortunately our neighbor Mr. Perrone was visiting relatives in Italy, and no one seemed to be watching from the nearby houses, so Winnie and I walked up his driveway and behind his house.

Two of them were together . . . and *that* was the problem. Small male dragonets never get along, and they were in the middle of a fight above Mr. Perrone's prize dahlias. Circling, then chasing each other in midair, the three-inch dragonets darted among the bushes like bossy hummingbirds—but dangerous, fire-breathing ones.

"I got them," Winnie said. Holding the book in her left hand, she swung the net down with her right.

The next instant, the mesh net disappeared in a small fireball.

"Whoa!" Winnie said as she dropped the shaft of the netless hoop.

Alas, now the dragonets had discovered a common enemy.

"Run, Winnie!" I said, and waved her over to me.

I didn't need to warn her not to move in a straight line. The clever girl already knew that would make it easy for them to hit her with their fire. Instead, she dodged to her left, then her right, all the time working her way back toward me.

When she ran past me, I darted forward, snatching first one angry warrior and then the other by the back of their necks. While I crossed the yard to the birdbath, I was careful to hold them at arm's length and face them away from me. As they angrily spit ribbons of flame into the air, they wriggled, trying to hit me with their fiery breath.

"Get ready," I told Winnie, and she crouched slightly with the book open, like a softball player catching a ball in her glove.

"Sorry about this, cousins," I whispered softly as I dunked them in the birdbath, dousing their flames. Wisps of smoke drifted skyward, and their damp wings splashed the water as they tried in vain to take to the air.

I drew the signs, and with a quick chant, they were restored to the book—not as they had been in the birdbath, but in all their glory in midflight . . . and midfight.

It had been a tiresome morning, to say the least. Winnie flopped on the grass. "What did I get us into?"

I felt my pet needed a little boost. "You did a marvelous job with their wings. When you take the time, you do lovely scales."

"Thanks," Winnie said with a sigh.

I counted our captured sketchlings—eighteen. Perhaps we were only missing one—the pemburu. I was confident it was hiding nearby like the others, and that if we put out a little magical something as bait, we could catch it easily. All in all, it had been a good morning's work—thanks to my partner in the hunt, Winnie.

It was nearly noon, and a pot of tea and something more substantial than a snack would be nice. "Let's take a short break for a proper lunch."

"I'll make sandwiches," Winnie said, grateful for a rest. She stood and picked up the remains of her net, and we walked back home.

"There should be some nice aged cheddar still in the icebox," I said. "Meet me downstairs in my apartment. I'll make a sweet currant tea to refresh us."

We parted ways by the kitchen, but before I reached my door, I remembered I hadn't told Winnie that I hated mayonnaise. So I went to the basement shelf where

Fluffy had kept her homemade chutney and brought a jar upstairs.

I was walking down the hallway when I heard myself say from the kitchen, "Winnie, let *me* hold the sketchbook while you make lunch."

Chapter Ten

*A pet who knows you and comes when you call
is both valuable and beloved.*

As quickly as words could work their magic, I was my dragon self again, and I rushed into the kitchen to see Winnie slipping the bag with the sketchbook from her shoulder. And reaching for it was my *identical twin*.

I had to admit that Winnie had done a very good job of capturing my alluring likeness. No sloppiness on my wings and scales and paws either.

No wonder Winnie had been so uncomfortable when I had asked her about sketch number twenty.

Winnie, oh, Winnie, what have you done? Did you really forget what the last sketch was, or were you simply afraid to tell me?

"No, you don't." I threw the chutney jar at the second Miss Drake and then leapt after it. The impostor was able to duck the jar . . . but not me.

The mansion's kitchen was large because Winthrop had loved to entertain anyone who interested him—and that was pretty much everyone. A gold prospector with mud still on his boots might be seated at dinner next to a wealthy banker from Germany or a diplomat from Abyssinia.

My twin and I crashed to the tiles and rolled back and forth, paw to paw, tails trying to lash the other, heads darting about as we lunged to bite the other's throat. I thought my experience at fighting would have given me the advantage. But as new a fighter as my twin was, we seemed to be evenly matched.

Then I heard the rumbling from my twin's body— not the rumbling of a hungry stomach, but the deeper noise of methane building in that special chamber before a dragon begins to spit out flame and destruction.

"Stop it! Stop it!" Winnie yelled, and I heard a bell begin clanging.

I twisted away from my twin to see a scared Winnie frantically beating a ladle against a huge metal lid. My bag and the sketchbook were once again on her shoulder, swaying with every *thump* and *clang*.

My twin got into a crouch. "Hurry. Open the book, Winnie, and I'll say the spell," she urged before I could.

How did she know the spell? Had she been hiding and observing us to see how we caught the other sketchlings? I remembered now the long shadow, the rustling bushes. I hadn't been able to detect her before because her scent was identical to my own! But could the sketchbook capture the original as easily as the copy? I didn't want to find out.

"Yes, open the book, but point it at that impostor," I said, nodding at the second Miss Drake. Now that Winnie could hear my voice, I hoped she'd notice my double's was a touch shaky from lack of practice.

"I'm the real Miss Drake," my twin insisted.

Winnie swiveled her head back and forth between my double and myself like someone watching a tennis match. "You both look so real." She pointed at me. "Are you *my* Miss Drake?" Then she turned. "Or are you?"

"I bought you a scarf at the same time as the sketchbook. Remember?" the faux Miss Drake wheedled. "Would the sketchling know that?" She spoke rapidly, reminding Winnie of other nice things that my pet and I had done together.

How had my twin learned all that? Did she have copies of my memories too?

The more my twin talked, the more confidence she gained and the more mellifluous and lilting her voice became—just like mine. She was sounding so convincing, I would have said she was me!

"Now please open the book, Winnie," my double finally said. "I'll say the spell, and we'll get rid of this sorry copy of me." Her wheedling voice grew sugary. "Be a dear."

Winnie took the book from the bag, but she didn't open it. Instead, she jerked her head at me. "Well, what do you say?"

I wasn't used to having a pet toy with me. "Don't be a goose. *I* am the one true Miss Drake."

Winnie smiled slyly as she flipped the book open, turned it so the open pages faced my double, and called to me. "Okay, do your stuff."

My twin panicked. "No! I know you're planning to trap the pemburu in there again. It'll get me when you do. Putting me back in the sketchbook is like putting a sheep into the same pen as a wolf."

"You're too big for it to eat," I said, beginning to move my paws in the magical passes.

"You weren't in the sketchbook with it, but I was, so I know its secret," my twin said urgently. "It's why all we sketchlings are afraid of it. That pemburu could even destroy San Francisco. Set me free and I'll tell you how."

It was risky to leave my double on the loose for many reasons, including the Agreement, but it was even riskier not to hear what she knew about the pemburu. "If we let you go, will you promise to leave the country?"

"Yes, yes." My twin gave a shudder. "Anything's better than returning to the book."

I lowered my paws. "Very well, then. If you'll tell me the secret, I swear on my honor that you will be free to go."

"I'll leave." Her elegant shoulders sagged in defeat. "What choice do I have?"

Winnie kept the book carefully aimed at her. "So what about the pemburu?"

My twin licked her snout with a forked tongue as

exquisite as mine. "The pemburu from the sketchbook grows larger and more powerful as it eats magic."

"What?" Winnie and I both said, shocked.

My twin had actually been crouching, waiting for the moment when this news would distract my pet and me. The next instant, she sprang, her powerful hind legs carrying her toward Winnie. There were pots and pans hanging from a rack suspended from the ceiling. They bonged and clanked as the scoundrel's head knocked against them.

She may have promised to leave the country, but she hadn't said anything about what she would do before she left—like trapping me in the book and taking it on her travels.

Any other human would have stood there frozen until the book was snatched from her. But Winnie was too quick-witted for that.

She threw herself forward and onto her back, sliding across the slippery tiles and under the leaping imitator's body and deadly hind paws. Rolling over on her side, she leaned on one elbow as she turned the book toward my twin.

"Now!" Winnie cried.

"I'll fix you, you brat!" My double sprang again, deadly claws stretching for Winnie, but the brave girl didn't flinch. She kept turning the open book so the pages could track her prey.

I broke all records saying the spell. My twin froze in midleap and began to shrink as she traveled through the air.

"No, no, don't send me back!" she cried, her voice growing higher and tinier with each moment until, with a zipping sound, she was caught on the page in the act of pouncing. I was glad she was as trim and slender as I was because she barely fit into the space as it was. Any larger and the book might not have been able to contain her.

Winnie rested her head against the tiles as she shut the book. "Whew, that was close."

I rose up to my full height, and I straightened my neck until my head brushed the high ceiling. I towered imposingly above her and looked her straight in the eyes. "Why didn't you say that you sketched me?"

She swallowed nervously as she stared up at me. "I finally worked up the nerve to tell you over lunch. But now it's too late. So"—her voice trembled ever so slightly— "are you mad?"

I relented. "Even if she was a copy, that sketchling's claws were sharp enough. It took a brave person to face her. So no, I'm not really angry." I added, "But you're still a goose."

"At least I'm a live goose," Winnie said.

I bent over and helped her to her feet. "How did you know I was the real Miss Drake?"

"It was her 'Be a dear,'" Winnie explained. "I knew a grouch like you would never say anything that icky."

"I think," I corrected, "you meant to say she lacked my fierce, independent spirit."

Winnie grinned. "Why don't you just admit that you're cranky?"

"I am *not* cranky," I sniffed. "I simply give you the benefit of my wisdom."

Winnie stowed the book back in the bag. "Well, can your wisdom tell if the fake Miss Drake was lying about the pemburu? Or do you think it really grows every time it eats magic?"

"For the moment, I think we have to assume that it does," I said. "It's too dangerous to ignore the warning."

"But even the fake Miss Drake was afraid of it, and she was your size," Winnie said, troubled. "Shouldn't you be afraid too?"

"If we can catch it before it eats too much, I should be safe enough," I assured her, but my stomach began to knot up with fear.

"And if we can't?" Winnie demanded.

I shrugged. "Then *no one* in San Francisco is safe."

And if I were a hungry pemburu, where would I go . . . ?

Winnie gnawed at her lip in frustration. "It could be anywhere in the city."

The horrifying truth slowly dawned on me. "Not just anywhere. The pemburu is a glutton. It will go where there's the most magic to eat."

Winnie wheeled around as she understood. "You mean . . . ?"

"Yes," I said grimly, already heading for the door, "the Enchanters' Fair—where there's enough magic for the pemburu to grow as big as a mountain."

Winnie gave a low whistle. "And then flatten San Francisco."

CHAPTER ELEVEN

*A bright pet is easily distracted at gatherings
large and small. A watchful eye and a quick paw
will keep your pet from wandering far.*

The Enchanters' Fair was
held in a hilltop park in
the western part of the city.
In the nineteenth cen-
tury, it had been a
cemetery near a
remote tip of the
San Francisco
peninsula.
Except for the
occasional ghost
playing pranks,

there were few visitors, and it had given magicals the privacy to display their talents in peace and see who was the most powerful.

But when the city had grown, the bodies were moved south to Colma, and the hilltop was converted into a neighborhood park. The Fair had also grown in size and scope so magicals could have fun with all sorts of races, contests, and shopping.

As we neared the Fair, a magical fog covered the hill like cotton batting. Thanks to spells that kept it hidden from prying eyes and ears—even more powerful than the one that kept me invisible—no natural could see what was going on. Much more powerful spells kept naturals from wandering into the park today.

"Are you sure it's here?" Winnie yelled from her perch on my back.

"As sure as that ridiculously tiny snout on your face," I said as I began to descend. "I founded the Fair, didn't I?"

Just in case any fairgoer was watching me, I landed light as a ginkgo leaf on the sidewalk. In the thick mist, I could barely see the set of steps leading into the park.

I wish there had been time to give my scales a good burnishing, but if wishes were horses and so on.

As soon as Winnie had dismounted, she ran around

in front of me. "What's wrong with my nose?" she demanded.

"Nothing that a little stretching couldn't help." I swung my mouth close to her ear and whispered, "But this is no time to be vain. Remember why we're here. If we're in luck, we'll catch the pemburu before it can do any more harm."

Sefa Bubbles knew how much I liked my elevenses, so years ago she had made a cunning pouch and attached it to my leg armor. The pouch's surface looked just like the real scales underneath it. I used to keep emergency snacks in it, but I'd found it was a convenient size for my cell phone.

I slipped it out now and checked it, but there was no text from Reynard yet. I had let him know what we were told about the pemburu to see if he could verify the tale. I could trust my geek friend to learn anything about anybody in some Internet cranny or other.

Together, Winnie and I mounted the damp steps. At the very top, the fog suddenly rippled as if a door had opened in the gray cloud. Through the opening, we could see magicals promenading about.

"Good afternoon, Miss Drake," Cullen said. All six and a half feet of him were packed with muscle, and his thick brown beard was decorated with small flowers.

He ran a nursery down in San Mateo and was one of the gentlest creatures until he gave himself over to his berserker's madness—the Rage, he called it. Then he was 350 pounds of killing fury almost impossible to stop.

As Marshal of the Fair, he had traded his rake for his ancient spear. The dark wooden shaft of the huge weapon was as thick as most humans' arms and decorated with runes of power. The blade was a foot long and shaped like a leaf, tapering to a point that Cullen claimed could cut the wind.

"We weren't sure you were coming," he said.

"I couldn't stay away after all," I told him. "This is my companion, Winnie."

Cullen leaned over to inspect her. "She looks like a biter. Has she had her shots?"

"Who are you—?" Winnie began indignantly.

I clamped a paw firmly over Winnie's mouth. "I'll answer for her behavior."

Cullen straightened. "Be it on your head, then, Miss Drake."

"Come along, Winnie, *dear*," I said through gritted fangs, and dragged her across the threshold of the barrier. "Rule number one for the Fair: Only pick fights you know you can win."

I stopped short. One whiff and I knew I had left behind the humdrum world outside. The pungent cinnamon of Serendip tickled my nostrils at the same time that honey cake from Araby soothed them. With so many magicals in one place, the very air crackled with power and made my scales tingle. A day at the Fair could leave a dragon feeling two centuries younger.

I was glad I had come, and even more glad I could show it to Winnie. After all, this was now her world too.

For once, Winnie was at a loss for words as we entered the bazaar. Merchants came from near and very, very far away to sell and trade here. Dust-colored djinns displayed their gems of power on floating carpets. Nigerian weavers sat at special looms blending spells and threads together into cloaks that would both stay dry in the rain and turn back any weapon. A jaguar shapeshifter transformed into amusing caricatures of his audience and then passed a bowl around for tips.

There were, of course, your usual groups of fire-eaters, sword swallowers, wand jugglers, dancing salamanders, synchronized flying pigs, and other entertainers.

"Fancy a treat?" I pointed a claw at a food booth where Kleodora the Siren was selling sun-gold apples dipped in Hyrcanian honey. The sight of them made me think of Fluffy again—she wouldn't leave the Fair each year before eating one, or even two, of them.

"What do the apples do?" Winnie asked as we headed toward the booth.

"They fill you up," I said. "Sometimes an apple is just an apple." But they were a very tasty treat as we began our search for the pemburu.

We ate them as we patrolled the Fair. Naturally Clipper was there with a selection of her favorite teas, silks, and sweets. A small tambour and fife floated in the air before her booth, playing a spritely jig. She had just sold some shampoo to a slothlike creature with moss growing in its fur.

Britomart stood guard in armor so shiny that it reflected the lights of the Fair like miniature suns. Her battle-ax, sharpened to a keen edge, was even shinier. She nodded to me as we walked over. "Glad you came, Miss Drake. It wouldn't be a proper Fair without you. Clipper thought you might change your mind, and she picked out a real nice prize for you when you win the Spelling Bee."

I felt a little pang of regret. Clipper always donated an exquisite tiara to the contest, but I had to keep to my true purpose. Leaning forward, I asked softly, "Anything unusual at the Fair?"

"Not a sign of a kobold or drought demon." Clipper grinned, misunderstanding. "Nor any ruckus reported . . . so far."

"That sketchbook—" Winnie began.

"Was of exceptionally fine quality," I cut her off. "You said you found it in a trunk. Do you know who the owner was?"

Clipper shook her head. "But he or she must have been a pack rat. There were all sorts of odds and ends in there. And I can't make heads or tails of any of them."

Clipper had an encyclopedic knowledge of magical paraphernalia and apparatuses. The items must be very obscure if she couldn't understand their purpose. But if they had wards as strong as the sketchbook's, they could be objects of power. I'd warn her later, after we dealt with the pemburu. With Reynard's help, I would identify the objects Clipper had and make sure they caused no harm.

"That pemburu of yours," I said as casually as I could. "What does it eat?"

"Magic," Clipper said. "That's why it's so good at detecting it. The collar keeps it from eating anything, though." She saw Winnie's frightened face. "But don't worry. When the shop closes, we feed it lots of lovely little magical scraps."

"And how big would it grow?" I asked.

Clipper pursed her lips. "I think I've heard about them growing as big as a basketball before they popped."

I breathed an inward sigh of relief because my double had been telling only half the truth.

There was a series of whistling roars from overhead, and I pointed so Winnie would see. Sam the Griffin whipped past, followed by Bergen, who liked to show off his wizardry. Today he was flying in a huge iron cauldron.

"I didn't think we'd be able to catch the flying races," I said, pleased. Flying with wings or by magic, the colorful contestants always delighted the crowds as they sought the Flying Dutchman Trophy.

Clipper raised her head. "This is the last heat before the actual race. Sam seems in good form, but my money's on Rhiannon. I saw her in an earlier heat. She was on a winged stallion that's a regular terror."

Rhiannon owned a stable and took care of naturals' regular horses as well as magicals' mounts.

"Let's hope the owner of the stallion never finds out," I said.

Clipper grinned. "Rhiannon will claim she was just exercising the beast."

I laughed. "That sounds like her." Bidding them good-bye, we walked away, but we hadn't gone more than four stalls when I heard the sound of a tiny hunting trumpet from my phone—the signal that Reynard had sent me a message, a text, and an email too. My old friend had done his research, and the news wasn't good. Flashing on and off on the screen were the words:

Big trouble!

Big Trouble!

BIG TROUBLE!

CHAPTER TWELVE

*Train your pet how to behave when meeting strangers
and their pets. No fighting, no biting, please!*

"What's wrong?" Winnie asked when she saw my face.

"Let me check," I said, and opened the email. Reynard had attached scans of two old drawings of pemburus to his email. One was the harmless common variety like Clipper's. It would eat magic until its belly burst. The other was a rare species not seen in thousands of years. It was rumored to be a real monster with an unusual appetite for magic. And it would keep growing as it ate!

I held the screen so Winnie could see too. Both had the same shape, but their colors were slightly different. I remembered the common one from Clipper's shop.

"That one looks like mine," she said, pointing to the other beast. "My green pencil broke, so I improvised with purple."

"Next time find the pencil sharpener," I told her.

So my double had been telling the whole truth after all. The pemburu at large was rare and ravenous for magic. No collar, if Winnie had even thought to draw one, would keep its appetite at bay. So rare, no one here had probably run across its like. Unless we caught it before it grew too large, vanquishing it would be a challenge.

I texted back to my friend: **Bad luck . . . it's the trouble-maker.**

And just as we turned down a new aisle, we had our first sign that the pemburu was indeed *here*.

A sorceress pointed at her pet gargoyle on its leash. Its body was as streamlined as a whippet, but it had a froglike head. "Ermintrude did not take a bite out of your cape."

"Your pet came sniffing at me." An angry dwarf held up a green cape with silver stars. There was a huge piece missing from the bottom. "And the next moment, I'm missing half of it."

Even if she had not been in her trademark purple velvet gown and black cloak, I would have recognized Silana just from the haughty way she curled her lip—dear Silana believed that manners were something everyone but she should have. "Sir, my Ermintrude would never eat an inferior weave such as that."

"Inferior?" the dwarf sputtered. "This is the finest invisible cape gold can buy."

The Fair is supposed to be a time of peace, but that doesn't mean feuds haven't started there. Whether it was Ermintrude or the pemburu who had stolen a snack, I thought I'd better step in.

"Gentle sir and gentle lady," I said, mentally crossing my claws when I used the latter term for Silana, "it would be a shame to spoil the day with a quarrel. As I am one of the founders of the Fair, it is my duty to preserve the spirit of amity and goodwill. So . . . what is your name, sir?" I glanced at the dwarf.

"Guntram," he said.

"Well, Guntram, please go to Clipper's booth and charge a new invisible cape to my account," I said.

"Clipper's, is it?" The dwarf rubbed his palms together in anticipation. "Now that's real high-class stuff."

As Guntram waddled off happily, Silana turned to me, trying to smile as politely as she could. "Ah, Miss Drake, and how are you going to beguile the judges this year?"

I wanted Silana to direct her anger at me rather than at the dwarf. I could defend myself against her spells, but the dwarf would find himself with green skin and a taste for flies.

"Oh," I said, trying to sound as casual as I could, "I thought I'd let someone else win this year."

Silana was almost too easy to tease. She began to fizz like a shaken-up bottle of soda. "LET someone else win!" She looked down when she heard the clinking sound. "Stop that!"

Winnie was rapping her knuckle against Ermintrude's forehead. "Hey, she's hollow inside."

I caught Winnie's wrist. Gargoyles are slow to react, but there was just the chance Ermintrude was feeling peckish, and a human hand would have made as good a snack as a cape. "You should always ask the owner's permission before you touch her gargoyle."

Silana tightened the leash, and Ermintrude whimpered as she was jerked closer to her mistress. "This urchin belongs to you?"

"This is my companion, Winnie," I said. "And, Winnie, this is Silana Voisin, High Sorceress and runner-up for Queen Bee for . . . How many years has it been, Silana? I've lost count."

"TOO many," Silana snapped, and with a tug at the leash, she stalked off with Ermintrude in tow.

"You made her run away without ever touching her," Winnie said admiringly. "Teach me to do that."

Putting my paw on Winnie's shoulder, I steered her in the opposite direction from Silana. "You're dangerous enough without extra lessons."

Every instinct screamed to hunt my quarry, to test the air for its scent and to search for tracks or other signs, but of course, I couldn't be that obvious. Under the guise of my showing the Fair to Winnie, we walked down each aisle—this one filled with booths where you could win all sorts of amazing tiny beasts if you could throw and land Ajax's battle-ax or Triton's spear on the bull's-eye. Winnie dawdled at one, listening to a barker invite her to toss a ball into one of many moving magic bowls to win a crystal-winged bird, dazzling with ever-changing colored lights. I knew she wanted to try, but I nudged her along.

"My dad always won me goldfish playing that game," she said softly.

"Next year," I whispered in her ear. "I promise."

Sadly today we had no time for games, for in the next aisle, a hair-restoring comb had disappeared. Three stalls down, a painting of a clown that told endless knock-knock jokes had vanished. What worried me was that each missing item was larger than the last. "It's growing," I murmured to Winnie.

"Then it should be easier to see," she said.

"You would think so," I said, frustrated. "But then why hasn't anyone seen it?"

Even as we hunted the pemburu, the events went on at the Fair. In addition to contests and races, there was also Magical Husbandry and its Best of Show contests—with various categories such as fur, fin, scale, and stone. (And no, I never entered any of my pets, as they deserved far more than blue ribbons.)

Usually there's a lot of ruckus from both pets and owners, but the noise was much louder than normal because things seemed to be missing—a collar, a brush, a staff, a mirror, and the like—all of them magical.

With all the accusations flying here and there, I wasn't surprised when a brawl broke out between two owners that sent one bystander, an unassuming juggler, head over teakettle, scattering his Japanese juggling bags every which way.

Watching the fisticuffs, I could feel the crowd grow

uneasy and enraged, so I didn't notice Winnie scrambling underfoot, gathering up the juggler's tools. But suddenly she stood up, tossed the colorful bags high, and began catching and juggling them herself. Then, as the juggler rose to his feet, she tossed them to him, and he, caught up in the spirit of play, tossed them back.

In a moment, both the quarrelers and the busybodies turned to watch the pair as they did their tricks. Finally Winnie tossed all the balls to him, and the juggler bowed to her as the crowd cheered. Spirits distracted and lifted, the quarrelsome mood had passed, at least for now, without any help from Cullen and his spear.

"Who taught you those tricks?" I asked Winnie as I herded her away.

"My dad. He loved to juggle," she said, then added proudly, "He was full of tricks."

And so are you, my pet. As she looked away, I saw how much a part of her he was and how very much she still missed him.

Suddenly a wave of magic spread through the Fair— the accidental result of many enchanters getting ready for the Bee. A magical spell is like a chord of music, but this was like an orchestra warming up: the notes all jumbled together, but the volume loud and large.

Overhead floated a football-size bee, one of the

magical constructs used for announcements at the Fair. "The Spelling Bee is about to begin at the Enchanters' Oval," boomed the voice. "Who will be the next Queen or King? Come and see."

If I could feel the magic, so could the pemburu.

Stooping, I swept Winnie into my forelegs. And unfurling my wings, I launched myself into the air.

I had to find that beast fast, before mischief turned into disaster.

CHAPTER THIRTEEN

There are tasks you and your pet can do together—
and some things you must do alone.

Even if I had been a stranger to the Fair, I would have known where the Spelling Bee was by the large crowd that had already surrounded the roped-in Oval.

As I angled down to the ground, the announcer said excitedly, "Wait!

Here's the Queen Bee herself making a dramatic appearance." It was Koyuske, a turtle-like kappa with a fringe of seaweed-like hair around the bald dome of his head. The red sash of a judge had been draped over his shell. "Has she decided to be a late entry?"

Koyuske was up in the judges' box. I hovered nearby. "Sorry, everyone!" I shouted. "We're just here to watch. But I lost track of the time and didn't want to be late."

This year, there were about thirty contestants listed on the entry board—twenty more than usual. Perhaps it was because with me gone, more enchanters thought they had a chance of winning.

While the others paced, muttering and waving their hands, Silana was using Ermintrude's back as a bench and yawning, as if bored. "Can you see any of *these amateurs* beating me?"

I looked around. "That's strange. There are usually some powerful enchanters competing every year, but all I see are newcomers."

Silana smiled slyly. "Yes, it's odd, isn't it?"

I knew Silana all too well. "Or did you bribe the usual contestants to stay away this year?"

Silana shrugged. "Bribery isn't against the rules."

"It isn't?" Winnie asked, puzzled.

"When I and my friends started the Spelling Bee," I

explained, "we decided that it would be in the *anything-goes* spirit of San Francisco. So there were no rules. As the Bee grew, we had to put in some minor procedural guidelines after a contestant forgot one year that the Bee is simply supposed to be fun and you weren't allowed to maim or kill your competition. But other than that, entrants are free to do what they want before and during the contest."

Ten years ago, five trolls had tried to kidnap me before the Bee. I had laid them out quickly enough, and Silana had cheerfully admitted to hiring them. I had told her it had been an insult to hire a mere five trolls and not to be so cheap the next time she tried to kidnap me. Trouncing her that year had been extremely satisfying.

"First up is Nynniaw the Wise," announced Koyuske, "with his Green Magic."

Clutching his cauldron of holly leaves, the druid strode into the Oval. There was a scattering of applause, but it wasn't very enthusiastic. Still, Nynniaw began an incantation in a pleasant, lilting voice, a charming spell of power that made even the grass in the performers' area begin to sway.

I laughed. "You're still being too cheap, Silana. You should have bribed him too."

As Silana began to scowl, Nynniaw's lilt turned to a frightened screech.

The pemburu had felt the power too—and was here to take it.

"Cullen," Koyuske called, "help us!"

I will say this for Silana. She might be treacherous, but she's no coward. When all the other enchanters stood frozen in fear, she ran toward the Oval, black cloak flying behind her. Ermintrude sprang after her.

"Stay here," I said to Winnie as I unfurled my wings. But she grabbed hold of my foreleg and wrapped her four limbs around it so she stuck to me tighter than a leech.

"I'm going with you," she said stubbornly. "I've got the book."

I didn't have a second to waste pulling her off me, so I swept over the stunned audience and into the Oval. I flew lower then so Winnie's feet could touch the ground. She let go as I rose slightly and hovered.

Nynniaw was on his knees, trying to hold on to his cauldron as it pulled away from him. But there was no sign of the pemburu itself.

Winnie raced in front of me and pointed. "Something's underground."

I whirled around and saw the small mound next to the cauldron.

Of course! That was how the pemburu had been sneaking about the Fair unseen. With a stroke of my wings, I sped ahead of Winnie.

But Silana had heard Winnie, too, and began moving her ivory wand and chanting even while she kept advancing.

"Silana, stop! You might hit Nynniaw!" I shouted.

"My aim is perfect," she yelled back to me. And with a flick of her wrist, Silana sent a bolt of lightning at the mound.

Fortunately Nynniaw's reflexes were as good as his magic. He let go of his disappearing cauldron and fell backward just in time. The grass on the mound flared into flame for a brief second as the lightning hit the spot. The smell of ozone was thick in my nostrils.

"Top THIS, anyone!" Silana cried in triumph.

But the next moment, her eyes widened and her shout became a howl. Lightning continued to fly from her wand into the ground, but it no longer charred anything. "Something's eating my magic!" Try as she might, she could not control her wand.

Burnt grass and blackened earth erupted upward when the pemburu's head appeared, its mouth twitching as it swallowed the lightning. Its body swelled even as it climbed out of the hole. The lobster-like creature was about the size of a small pony as it stood on its many legs, hissing and spreading wide its pincer claws.

Silana stumbled forward. "Help me! My hand's stuck to my wand!"

With a growl, Ermintrude leapt toward the pemburu, her mouth opening to reveal rows of fangs—and she vanished.

"Noooooooooooo!" Silana wailed.

A few of the contestants had worked up enough nerve to come into the Oval, and there were many more enchanters in the crowd. Even Nynniaw had begun to draw a magical diagram in the dirt as he started to chant.

Putting a paw on Winnie's head, I shoved her down against the grass with me as the first spells began flying.

More magic smashed against the pemburu—some of it was visible as lightning, but the rest could only be heard or smelled.

Of course, the magic only fed the pemburu, so it kept growing and growing until it was the size of an elephant. Its armor of overlapping plates made it look like an ancient Japanese warrior. And it was still expanding. I gave up any idea of using my fire on it.

"Stop, you idiots," I yelled. "Your magic is only feeding it and making it larger."

The more sensible enchanters halted their spells, but

others either hadn't heard me or were too worked up and continued to shoot magic at the pemburu until it was the size of three elephants.

They only gave up when Koyuske began booming over the announcing bees, "Cease and desist. Give Cullen the Hero room to work."

Cullen strode across the field, shaking his spear angrily. "I am Cullen of the Spear," he announced, already working up the Rage. "Why are you trying to ruin the Fair? I hate monsters like you. You take. You destroy."

Winnie pulled the sketchbook from her bag. "Stop him, Miss Drake. We can catch that thing."

"I'm afraid it's too large to fit into the book now," I said. There were limits to how much magic you could cram into a small volume of space.

"We can't let Cullen take on that thing with just a spear," Winnie said. "He needs a machine gun at least."

"That spear is a weapon of power," I told her, "and, in Cullen's hands, far deadlier than any gun."

"Does that mean the spear is magic?" Winnie asked.

Immediately I reared up. "Cullen, stop! Go back!" And Winnie added her voice to mine.

When Cullen turned his head and I saw his dazed eyes and his mouth twisted into a scowl, I knew the Rage had already claimed him.

"Cullen, that thing eats magic," I warned. "Your spear will be just a snack."

A little spark of consciousness must have remained because he nodded jerkily. But instead of retreating, he raised his spear and jammed the blade deep into the dirt. From his belt, he pulled a knife. The words rasped from him as he grinned. "Then it's cold steel."

What could that puny knife do against the pemburu's armor? But when Cullen was in the Rage, he knew only one thing: Attack!

"Stop!" I yelled, but Cullen gave himself completely to the Rage. Howling his war cry—*"Nemain! Nemain!"*—he charged. Flowers flew from his beard as he ran.

It would take a dragon to make Cullen halt now, and I broke into a gallop. I was still fifty feet away when he reached the pemburu. The monster swept a claw toward him with a sound like a wind rushing through the trees. As the pincers closed with a loud *clack*, Cullen threw himself to the grass, rolled beneath them, and then bounced back to his feet.

A cheer went up from the crowd. Everyone had stayed to watch as if this was all being staged for their entertainment.

Cullen's arm shot forward like a piston, but the knife's tip simply skidded across the pemburu's plates with a screech like a fingernail on a blackboard.

Cullen danced back and forth as he dodged the pemburu's claws. He tried to thrust his knife between the plates, but the pemburu twisted its body and the trapped blade broke. The next moment, a blow from a claw sent Cullen sprawling on the ground.

A groan went up from the crowd then, and from the corner of my eye, I saw Silana and some of the magicians beginning to edge away. In a few seconds, the panic would spread to the crowd, and someone was bound to get trampled as everyone tried to escape.

Neither magic nor brute force could defeat the pemburu. I might be able to capture it if I could swell to an enormous size, but because I was surrounded by spectators, I couldn't grow too large without crushing someone.

And then I realized we were all making the same mistake. We needed to stop the pemburu, not beat it in a battle. And size was the key to ending the threat.

As I pounded over the last fifty feet of grass, I began to work my spell.

"Come back!" Winnie shouted.

The pemburu whirled at her cry and saw me. Immediately its huge claw slashed through the golden haze that surrounded me, and the pincers snapped shut where my head had been.

I heard Winnie give a cry of agony. "Miss Drake!"

The pemburu had struck too late. I'd already shrunk to the size of a fly. As the haze cleared, the monster now seemed as tall as a pagoda.

The giant pemburu whipped its eyestalks about frantically as it tried to find me, but I was too small now—a speck, but a dragon nonetheless. Behind me, I heard Winnie crying as if her heart was breaking. I wanted to shout to her that I was all right, but she would never have heard my tiny voice.

Growing desperate, the pemburu began to swing its claws back and forth, churning up the air and tumbling me about as if I was being blown by the winds of a mighty hurricane.

I landed hard against one of its armor plates, which now seemed as big as a truck. I tried to dig my claws into the smooth surface but wound up slipping and sliding across it. So instead, I let my momentum carry me to the edge. Grabbing the lip in my forepaws, I curled my body and inserted myself neatly in the crevice between two overlapping plates of its armor.

The pemburu went wild then, spinning and twisting as it searched for me. Now I felt as if I was in a ground-shaking earthquake, bouncing up and down between the plates like a rubber ball. Its legs must have kicked up the field into a cloud of dirt because the dust puffed into my hiding space.

I had to stop the pemburu before it began rampaging and hurt someone, especially Winnie.

So I edged deeper into the blackness. Somewhere ahead was its soft inner flesh, and buried within that was its heart.

As the poet once sang, *Deadly is the darkness. Deadlier is the dragon in the dark.*

When I bit into the pemburu's heart, it died and all the magic it had devoured suddenly devoured *it,* and so its vast body disappeared with one great *BOOM!* I wound up plopping on my back on the ground, stunned. It was so silent at first that I thought the crowd had fled. I would have liked to catch my breath, but I heard Winnie shouting, "Miss Drake, where are you?" She sounded so sad and scared that I immediately panted out the transformation spell and began to grow to my normal size again.

Clipper was there with a conscious Cullen. So was Britomart, who had been holding Winnie at a safe distance from the pemburu, but when Winnie saw me, she broke free. "I thought you were dead."

"At times . . . so did I," I puffed.

With a leap, Winnie wound her arms around my neck and hugged me. "Don't ever do that again."

"I don't . . . intend to," I said. "Now let go . . . of me. I'm a mess. You'll . . . ruin your clothes."

"You're a corker, Miss Drake, a corker," Cullen said, shaking his head in admiration as the crowd roared and roared.

In all the years I had been winning the Spelling Bees, I'd never heard anything like that. At first, I thought they were cheering in relief because the pemburu was dead.

But then Nynniaw began to chant, "Miss Drake." The other enchanters picked it up and soon the whole crowd was shouting my name rhythmically.

"Take a bow, Miss Drake," Clipper urged.

"I'd rather take a bath," I growled back.

"Oh, don't be such a grouch," Winnie scolded.

So I nodded to the crowd and managed to lift a foreleg in a feeble wave.

Winnie put her hands beneath the knee joint to keep my foreleg up. "You're going to have to do that for your fans on all four sides."

"You're enjoying . . . bossing me around far too much," I complained.

"Yup," Winnie agreed. "Now let's try to turn."

I managed to acknowledge each part of the crowd around the Oval. "There. Satisfied?"

Suddenly Koyuske's voice boomed over the announcing bees. "Attention, everyone. We all know how much Miss Drake has already done for the magical community. Today, we are even deeper in her debt for saving us from a monster that was proof against magic and weapons. So for this tremendous feat, I think Miss Drake deserves to be the Queen of the Fair yet again. What say all of you?"

This time the cheers rolled across the hilltop like thunder.

Chapter Fourteen

Expect your pet to do the unexpected.

I slept very late the next day, and I imagined that Winnie had also. I didn't see her or hear her knocking at my door, which was just fine with me. I needed time to restore myself with a good book, some tea, and more than a little quiet.

After dinner, I placed my new tiara in the cedar chest along with the others I had won over the years. This one was quite delicate, with rows of brilliant red tourmaline. Clipper had selected well. It had looked quite charming against my flame-colored scales. In the lamplight, all the tiaras gleamed, reminding me of many happy conquests.

But I was in the mood now to tidy up, not reminisce, after the challenges of the past week. I tried to shut the lid, but the chest was very full. I had to rearrange the tiaras before I could close it. Perhaps I would ask Silana if she knew where I could buy a larger chest.

I was still imagining Silana's expression when I noticed that Winnie had left her precious sketchbook behind. That was a surprise. I flipped through it quickly just to make sure that everyone was still in its proper place, and the magic intact, when I saw something unexpected.

Two pages had been ripped out. I was sure they had been there before the contest, and maybe even after it. But they were missing now.

I could feel my heart racing like a Roman charger. *Who had stolen them? Was it done at the Fair? But how?*

Questions whirled around in my mind. But my heart knew the answer before my head did.

Winnie!

There wasn't time to lose. I had to find out what she was planning before she stumbled into a worse disaster. *But why? Why? WHY?* Winnie knew the trouble she could cause with those pages. What would make it so worthwhile that she would risk the magic again? What secret wish was tempting her now?

Oh no, my pet! I suddenly realized what she could be planning and knew I had to stop her . . . before it was too late.

"Oh, Winnie," I whispered as I stepped out of my rooms with the sketchbook. I set it down on the floor and shrank myself to the size of a parrot. "Be careful what you wish for."

With the sketchbook in my claws, I sped through the basement and up the stairs. The kitchen was dark, but I knew the placement of every hanging pot, so I darted between them.

Why did I keep trying to raise humans as pets? It was always the same. They knew they shouldn't do something, but they did it anyway. Try as I might to guide them, I was never really able to train them to do what was best and safest for them.

So often all I could do was clean up the mess afterward. All the aggravations and disappointments had surely stolen centuries from my life. I should never have taken on Winnie as a pet. She was proving to be the most challenging one yet.

But dipping around the dining room chairs, I remembered all the candlelit dinners where Fluffy and I had discussed so many wondrous things of past and present. And I knew that I couldn't help myself. I still wanted to believe in Winnie and her promise . . . with a bit of dragon help. So clean up the mess, I would.

I darted along the center hall and up the stairway to the bedrooms on the second floor. Her door was slightly ajar, and I zigzagged through the doorway into what had once been Fluffy's private retreat. Oh, I remembered this room so well—the high ceiling, the view of the bay. Even when I was my own size, this was a delightfully spacious place to be.

Fluffy's favorite patchwork quilt was still on her bed when I flew over it and then her desk, but the pages were not in sight. Neither was Winnie. Perhaps I had been wrong.

Then I remembered the alcove—Fluffy's secret spot. Tucked at the back of a deep closet was a seat along a bay window, where one could sit and watch the ships sail into the harbor. It was a good place to hide, undisturbed and unseen.

I glided between the rows of dresses and coats and saw my Winnie, curled up on the seat.

The two pages were lying on the cushions by her feet, and her pencils were on her lap. She was staring out the window as if she was trying very hard to see or imagine something . . . or someone.

I grew as large as I could to comfortably fit in the space. "Winnie," I called. "I think we need to talk."

"Oh," she said, turning to me as if she was coming back from some place or time far away.

"Are those pages from your sketchbook, Winnie?" I asked. "You haven't drawn on them yet, have you?"

"I did," she said softly, "but then I erased them, or most of them."

She stared at me, and her face was etched with sadness. "I knew I shouldn't, but I couldn't help myself," she said, and she began to cry.

If I were a human, I might have hugged her, but it is not easy for a dragon to show compassion, except to be nearby and listen.

"It will be all right, Winnie," I said, softening my voice. "Whatever is wrong, we can fix it."

What did you wish for? What did you draw? I wondered, afraid of the answers.

I took a step so I could see the drawings. Even erased,

I could recognize the features she had drawn. On one, there was a jolly-looking man, young and tanned, Winnie's father. And on the other was, oh my, Fluffy, drawn from a photo but as real as I could remember her.

As I understood what she had done, my eyes filled with tears and my heart filled with compassion for the girl. She had wished to have her father alive again and to have Fluffy back for me.

Magic is like that sometimes. It takes your dearest wish and tempts you to play with it. But capricious and unfeeling, it is simply playing with you to see what you will do. To see what you are made of. Everyone who ever deals with magic faces times of testing, and this was ours.

For as much as Winnie was yearning to bring her father back, I suddenly realized how much I would love to have Fluffy in my life again. Oh, how I had missed her. And with my magic, I could help Winnie make her sketches close to the originals, and full-size to boot. I knew it would be a challenge, but I thought I could do it. A child should have her father. . . .

"I just wanted him to hold me," said Winnie, sobbing now. "I miss him so much."

"I know, Winnie," I whispered, moving closer to her. She slid from the bench and wrapped her arms around my neck, our heads touching. We both sobbed until there were no tears left; we were worn out, and pearls bounced and scattered, clicking on the parquet floor.

And that made us laugh.

"You are a messy crier, you know," Winnie said, snuffling.

"Well, at least something good comes from my tears," I answered back.

But something good came from that cry besides pearls. We had both released much of the sadness that we were feeling, and the sadness we shared bound us together even more.

"You know you shouldn't bring your father back," I said. "Just as I know I shouldn't bring back Amelia . . . no matter how much I would like to. It would be selfish of me and a dishonor to the person she was."

"I know," she said. "That's why I erased my sketches . . . just as soon as the edges started to glow. I needed to think it over more. . . . I figured if I changed my mind, I could always redraw them."

"And now?" I asked her.

"You better put them back in the sketchbook," she said. "Before I do change my mind."

"I have a better idea," I told her. "Let's give all the sketchlings a fond farewell and a moment of glory."

We left the closet, and I asked her to close the drapes

and turn out the lights. I grew to my full size, motioned her to sit beside me, and placed the sketchbook between us.

"It's time to release these creatures in a way that will do no harm yet will set their spirits free."

I had been working on this spell off and on through the years, refining it, and I thought I could add something that would be lovely too.

I began by chanting the spell that would make what was magic no longer so. I suspected that this book had once been very, very powerful, more powerful than the one who was using it. Removing magic has to be done very carefully, and I felt that someone had tried to do so in haste. The book had been drained of much of its power, but not all.

Now was the time to complete the task.

I moved my paws back and forth as if I was sweeping away dust instead of magic. As I spoke the last words of the spell—*"Aikare! Aikare! Aikare!"*—the book rose in the air and the pages began to flutter. But rather than a golden glow, the book glowed red. I continued the chant until the color changed, fading, and the draining of power began. I waited as it floated between us, and then I began another

141

chant, lighter and more carefree. The book turned to the page where a blue dragonet was on guard.

"Release and return," I said, and the page flared and crumpled as a blue streamer of light shot upward to the ceiling. Just below the chandelier, the light burst into a thousand smaller lights, painting the tiny dragon's picture above our heads in a mosaic of colored sparks. It raised its head and spit flames, revealing the spirit every dragonet should have, and then . . . the lights showered down over our heads like a shimmering fireworks display. The dragonet was gone.

"Ahhhh," said Winnie. "It was so beautiful."

"Yes," I said. "It had a magnificent spirit, and now it is free."

One by one, I called the creatures' names and the book released them, and as it did so, it lost a bit more of its power and its magic. Each soared high, glowed brightly and colorfully, and then vanished in a shower of fluttering lights.

The lizards, sirens, moths, and dragonets were freed in a display that took our breath away again and again.

The mini-pteranodon stretched its wings across the entire ceiling, as large as any ancient pteranodon that ever sailed the skies. And just as the gigantic beast glimmered and faded, a tiny bright meteor streaked downward and hit the wooden floor with a sharp *clink*.

"My medal!" cried Winnie, and she scooted over to scoop up her great-grandfather's medal, once lost and now found.

I couldn't help thinking, with some pleasure and a touch of sadness, too, how much Fluffy would have enjoyed seeing her study filled with such an amazing spectacle.

It took us some time, but finally the book was blank again. There was hardly any glow left. All the characters inside it had been freed.

Winnie was holding the last two pages. She didn't say anything but gave them to me. I placed the one with her father on top of the book, and let her call his name as I recited the releasing spell.

The page glimmered red and then turned into a sparkling flare that sped up, brighter and faster than the others. It spread across the ceiling, and her father's shining face grinned merrily at Winnie. I could sense so much of Winnie in him and saw the cleverness, stubbornness, courage, and curiosity in him that she loved. And then, with a wink of his eye, his face dissolved into a lovely shower of green and yellow lights. Winnie stood, arms held high, letting the lights shine over her face, smiling a smile I hadn't seen before.

I was a bit selfish in saving Fluffy for last, but if so, who could blame me? As I placed her page on the book, the faint indentations of Winnie's drawing began to glow pink and yellow, the color of the petals of tea roses, Fluffy's favorites.

A bright pink spark soared high, and her face glimmered over our upturned ones. She smiled, or so it seemed, at both of us before gently rippling and then dissolving into a cascade of pale pink petals, like cherry blossoms drifting on a windy spring day in Golden Gate Park.

When I finished my chant, the book turned dark and dropped, with a *thump*, on the floor. As I touched it, I felt no tingling, no sensation at all. The magic was gone now. It was a sketchbook like any other, but with a prettier cover—and with fewer pages than before.

"That was the right thing to do," said Winnie. "Wasn't it?"

"Yes," I said. "It was the right and loving thing to do."

We sat in the dark room for a moment or two, remembering and savoring the presence of our loved ones and their spirits, which would always glow inside us.

Then I pulled open the drapes so we could see in the dark room, but not be seen. The real lights of the city drew us back into the everyday world again.

Winnie was good about picking up all the pearls and putting them in a little bag.

"That should pay for quite a lot of tea and crackers," she said, giving them to me.

And some tuition, I thought, but now wasn't the time to be talking about school. Not on a special night like this.

Instead, I rose and whispered her a good night, wishing, "Sweet dreams, Winnie."

In three shakes of a dragon's tail, I was the size of a bee, whizzing through the dark rooms I knew so well and into my own home and my own bed, myself again.

And whether it was my wish fulfilled or simply the release of the magical ones, we both slept better than we had in a long time, full of pleasant dreams with the ones we loved.

CHAPTER FIFTEEN

Is a pet worth the trouble? Absolutely! When you bond with your pet, she will love you despite your warts— and if you're lucky, sometimes because of them.

"Do you want this?" Winnie asked the next day, tossing the sketchbook on my sofa. "It may be safe now, but I don't want to use it anymore."

"I'll trade you," I told her, offering her my new tiara. I had decided that after last night she deserved it. With a little adjustment here and there, the delicate crown fit her perfectly, and she twirled around so I could see it from all angles.

"Stunning," I told her. "Simply stunning."

When she stopped spinning, she put her

hand in her pocket and looked surprised. "Oh, I forgot, this is yours," she said. "I found it inside a shoe."

The pearl was an especially lovely one, reflecting the depths of sadness and affection I had felt the night before. It would bring an exceptional price. As large as any Tahitian pearl, this gem of mine was blue-black with a rainbow luster. The highlights opalesced from green to purple to pink as I rolled it in my paw.

"I think you should keep it," I told her. "You were wise and brave last night, and I would like you to have it as a gift from me."

"Thanks," she said, pausing. "My dad would have loved painting the colors in this."

It was a gift freely given, yet one I might one day regret. I was feeling too carefree this morning to be as cautious as my elders taught me to be.

"What are we going to do today?" Winnie asked brightly, as if she was expecting me to amuse her with my latest trick.

"Well, we could race the djinn on a flying carpet in Samarkand. Or we could go to Venice and ride with the Cat Doge as he sails his sky gondola just above the fireworks," I told her. "But I think today we'll get your school supplies. Remember, classes start next week."

She tried to make the best of the situation. "At Clipper's?"

"No, at stores that naturals run," I said, and I could see her slump with disinterest. But I knew she would soon get out of her little snit.

Since my favorite stationery store was in Sausalito, we could take the California Street cable car and then walk over to the Ferry Building and catch the ferry across the bay. So I planned a fun outing I knew she would enjoy.

Yesterday was summer, foggy and overcast. Today, you could feel fall ready to make its appearance. As soon as all the pesky summer tourists left, San Francisco paid back the natives with the finest weather of all.

Sun and light surrounded us, and the bright blue sky seemed to leap from the deep gem-blue waters of the bay. Though it was warm enough on land, there is always a good breeze on the ferry, so I had suggested Winnie wear an extra sweatshirt. I put on a herringbone jacket with a design that reminded me of interlocking scales. Yet not even the gusty West Wind was going to force Winnie to take off her tiara. She wore it proudly, with a hand holding it firmly in place.

Her other hand fingered the medal hung once again around her neck. "There's a dent here where the pteranodon bit it," she said, lifting it to show me.

"I can fix that," I told her, "with a few strokes of a goldsmith's hammer or a bit of magic, if you like."

"No thanks," she said. "This way when I touch it, I won't ever forget what happened—even when I'm old."

"Well, we'll stop by a jeweler I know and pick up a silver chain for it."

"A cord's fine with me," she said with a jut of her chin.

I was sure it was, but some of the girls at school, especially the privileged naturals, might not agree.

"Of course, cord has character," I said, "but your great-grandfather's medal is too much of a treasure. It deserves something finer."

And we found just the perfect chain at my friend Felisa's boutique near the ferry landing in Sausalito. Sweet Felisa cooed over the old pendant, warming Winnie and delighting her with a woven silver necklace, comparable to the finest any elfin craftsman could make.

"It does look nicer now," Winnie said. "Thank you."

"You're most welcome," I said. "Now for those school supplies."

At the stationer's shop, Anthony helped us find everything we needed, including a new, blank, and decidedly unmagical sketchbook that Winnie carefully selected. When the total was rung up, Winnie tugged at my arm and whispered, "You don't have to buy me all this school stuff. How are you going to pay for it—in pearls?"

"No," I told her, "with my bank debit card."

I may be old-fashioned in some things, but I can be au courant when necessary. "And I know I don't have to buy your school stuff, but I want to."

On the way back, we stood in the bow of the boat, wordless and windswept, so we could enjoy the view of San Francisco growing closer and closer—the tall skyscrapers lining downtown, the hills of the city behind them, so many lovely buildings and places I loved and wanted to share with Winnie. I thought I could see even the three dragons rampant swirling from our turret just as the boat touched one of the docks outside the Ferry Building.

"Shopping makes me thirsty," I said as we unpacked our purchases at home.

"And hungry," added Winnie.

She set the table, and I spread out the treats we had chosen from the vendors at the Ferry Building Marketplace. Crackers baked in Monterey, cheeses from Marin, fruits from Sonoma, and chocolates made in the city and Burlingame were our treasures today.

I filled our tumblers with sparkling apple cider, and we toasted.

"To adventures past," I said with pride.

"And adventures yet to come," Winnie continued.

"May they be merry and a little less hazardous," I added.

We enjoyed our feast until it was time for Winnie to leave.

"See you tomorrow," she called.

"Yes, my pet," I said after she was gone. Then I re-filled my glass and toasted one last time, wishing, "To new friends and a new school year too."

Before I went to bed, I was determined to finish tidying up. There were dishes to wash and dry and that trouble-some sketchbook to put away. I flipped through the pages one last time, and to my surprise, there was one grand sketch spreading across the center pages. Clever girl, she knew I wouldn't miss it.

"Oh, Winnie!" I said. "Good job!" I smiled at the drawing she had done for me to see and to keep. Then I shut the book and tucked it between Shakespeare and Plato. But the scene stayed in my mind until I drifted off to sleep.

It was my room, complete with rug, sofa, and music box, where two friends, both wearing colorful tiaras, were playing a game of checkers and drinking tea. Underneath, in bold and fancy letters, Winnie had carefully printed:

Miss Drake and Me